Thank You For Not Shifting

RENEE GEORGE

I0544886

A PARANORMAL MYSTERY ROMANCE BOOK

WWW.PECULIARMYSTERIES.COM

Thank You For Not Shifting

Peculiar Mysteries Book 3

Copyright © Renee George 2016

All rights reserved. No part of this publication may be reproduced, stored in a retrieval system, or transmitted, in any form or by any means, without the prior permission in writing of the copyright holder.

Any trademarks, service marks, product names or named features are assumed to be the property of their respective owners, and are used only for reference. There is no implied endorsement from the author of this work.

This is a work of fiction. All characters and storylines in this book are inspired only by the author's imagination. The characters are based solely in fiction and are in no relation inspired by anyone bearing the same name or names. Any similarities to real persons, situations, or incidents are purely coincidental.

Cover Art: Renee George

First Print Edition: August 2017

ISBN-13: 978-1-947177-03-1

ISBN-10: 1-947177-03-6

0 9 8 7 6 5 4 3 2 1

Welcome to Peculiar, Missouri!

Chavvah Trimmel, a werecoyote and part owner in Sunny's Outlook, has recovered physically from her kidnapping, but emotionally she still has scars. Her best friend Sunny is happily married and knee deep in baby poop, all Chavvah wants to do is focus on the future and forget about the past. When the Tri-State Council of therianthropes decides to hold their annual Jubilee in Peculiar, Chavvah is stoked. It's great for business, and a hunky new shifter in town might be the answer to getting over a crush she has on a certain werewolf shaman-doctor who doesn't know she even exists.

A murder in Sunny's Outlook makes ignoring Billy Bob Smith impossible, especially after he insists on trying to keep her safe. But his strange behavior--acting protective, territorial, and annoyed (okay, the annoyed part isn't that strange), has Chavvah worried more about her heart than her safety. It doesn't help that she's hearing voices...again.

The town, full of shifters from Arkansas, Kansas, and Missouri, is on lock down. Another murder has everyone on edge. Can Chavvah and her friends find the killer? Or will she or someone she loves be the next victim?

Paranormal Mysteries and Romances

By Renee George

Peculiar Mysteries
www.peculiarmysteries.com
You've Got Tail (Book 1)
My Furry Valentine (Book 2)
Thank You For Not Shifting (Book 3)
My Hairy Halloween (Book 4)
In the Midnight Howl (Book 5)

Barkside of the Moon Mysteries
www.barksideofthemoonmysteries.com
Pit Perfect (Book 1)
The Money Pit (Book 2)
Pit & Run (Book 3)

Witchin' Impossible Mysteries
www.romance-the-night.com
Witchin' Impossible (Book 1)
Witchin' Impossible: Rogue Coven (Book 2)
Witchin' Impossible: Familiar Protocol (Book 3)
Witchin' Impossible: Mr. & Mrs. Shift (Book 4)

Dedication

For Robbin.

I couldn't do any of this without you.

CHAPTER 1

THE COWBELL OVER the entrance to Sunny's Outlook jangled for the umpteenth time. I heard the waiter, Jo Jo, offer a welcome, so I continued scrubbing off the diner table and re-setting it. *Oo-wee.* I was tired. Who knew being co-owner of a vegetarian restaurant in a tiny shifter town would be so exhausting?

Not me.

The breakfast crowd had been full of eager beavers. Not real beavers, of course, though werebeavers do exist, some were even in town this week, but most of their kind tended to be integrators—therians who hid their second natures to live like non-shifters. My parents are integrators, which means Mom is seriously unhappy with my brother Babe and me for living in an (almost) therian-only locality. Dad is more rational about the situation, but he shows his disapproval in other ways.

A blond boy ran inside the door, he was laughing as a teenage girl, face red with fury, fought to catch him. The boy was my friend Ruth Thompson's nine-year-old son Linus, and the girl was his nineteen-year-old sister Michele.

"Linus," Michele scolded. "You hold it right there."

The boy dropped to his hands, and in seconds, he transformed into a young buck, nubs for horns and the softest looking buff-blond fur.

"Linus!" my best friend and business partner Sunny shouted. "No shifting in the restaurant. This is a shift-free zone, boy."

Michele blushed as Jo Jo Corman, our young waiter, wrangled the small deer wearing denim shorts and a pale blue tank top.

"I'm so sorry, Sunny. You too, Chav," Michele said. She grabbed the shorts off the ground when they fell down the deer's bony legs. In one of the pockets, she pulled out a phone. "Got it!" She held it up triumphantly then blushed again. "Linus stole it out of my hands while I was texting." She gave Jo Jo a meaningful look.

A silly grin formed on his face until he saw me staring, then he blushed as well. Over the past year, he'd let his short, brown hair grow out a couple of inches and wore it spiked with blue frosted tips. I wasn't sure whether it was any better than the blond leopard spots that used to grace his head. The spots had really pissed his dad off to no end. Though, Brady Corman had preferred the dyed hair to all of Jo Jo's tattoos and piercings. I think Jo Jo told me once that he had twenty-six piercings in all. Twelve of them were in his face. I really didn't want to know the location of the others.

"Michele, you better get your brother out of here and take his shorts with you." I looked at the deer who I could swear was silently laughing. "Don't you dare shift back in here, Linus. No flashing your wee-willy in the restaurant. Take it outside."

He snorted then pranced to the door, the pale blue tank top tight against his chest. He was already growing into a young adult. I'd known the youngest Thompson since he was six, and it just didn't seem possible he was already starting to grow horns. It made me feel old.

Michele opened the door for him. She gave a shy wave to Jo Jo, and he nodded to her.

"Oh my," Sunny said. She danced around Jo Jo like a fairy throwing flower petals. "I think young love is in the air."

"Stop it," Jo Jo said. He looked at me, his eyes pleading. "Chavvah, help me."

I grinned. "I think I hear a baby crying. Do you hear a baby crying, Jo Jo?"

"No, Chav," Sunny pleaded.

Jo Jo's expression faltered, then he smiled. "I wonder if Baby Jude's hungry."

"I hate you," Sunny exclaimed. She covered her chest with her forearms, but it didn't hide the breast milk streaming in twin rivers down her pale green blouse. She headed toward the bathroom where she kept spare shirts.

"That wouldn't happen if you'd wear breast pads," I muttered.

I returned to my post behind the counter. We'd been doing a brisk business due to the Tri-State Council July Jubilee. This was the first time Peculiar had hosted the annual event, and our therianthrope community had been overrun by shifters from the surrounding states. Right now, our part of the Ozarks was bursting with every type of shifter you could imagine.

The cowbell over the entrance of Sunny's Outlook jangled for the umpteenth time. Delbert and Elbert Johnson, the twins who ran the general store across the street, came inside.

"Hey, guys," I said. "Just grab an open table. I'll be with you in a minute."

"No hurry, Chavvie." Delbert grinned, his forehead crinkling over bright blue eyes. He was so cute for an old possum.

"Take your time, darlin'. We're not going anywhere," Elbert added.

They both had that Uncle Jesse look. You know, the dude from Dukes of Hazzard. White hair, white beards, overalls, and a little tubby in the middle. I could tell them apart by only two things, Delbert had a thinner face, and Elbert had a small freckle near the corner of his left eye. Sunny had actually pointed it out. At a distance, it was nearly impossible to see the difference, but up close it was no problem.

The cowbell jangled again. I ignored it while I finished recording the last order.

"Chavvah."

I immediately recognized the deep male voice.

My heart jumped into my throat, and my palms turned clammy and cold.

Ugh. I hated myself. *You are not a teenager. Stop acting like one.*

I looked up and met the smoky gray eyes of Dr. Billy Bob Smith, the local witch doctor and family medical practitioner. I went completely squishy inside. He was the most gorgeous man I'd ever laid eyes on. Usually, he wore his hair down in silver waves that flowed over his shoulders. Right now, he wore it tied back, really showing off his angular face with a strong but narrow jaw, a wide mouth, straight, broad nose, and hypnotizing eyes.

Once, he'd had a tangle of thick dreadlocks down to his trim waist. I still remembered how soft his hair felt when he'd carried me bloodied and bruised away from the hunters who'd tried to kill me. I lost myself for a moment thinking about the how the doc's hair had brushed my skin like the tips of angel wings, and even though I'd been in excruciating pain, I'd been comforted.

Billy Bob was good at offering comfort.

But he was a lycanthrope, and I was a werecoyote. We were about as compatible as lemon juice and an open wound.

There wasn't a person in town who didn't sing the doc's praises—except me, of course. He had a medical degree from a big university. Yet, he also believed in hoodoo spiritualism or what he called, "earth magic."

I couldn't see how he could possibly reconcile science and magic.

"Did you hear the one about the wolf who walked into a diner and was ogled by a coyote?" Elbert Johnson chuckled.

Jo Jo laughed.

I closed my gaping mouth and snapped at Jo Jo, "Don't you have work to do?"

He walked away with a wide grin on his pierced lips, and I caught the fist bump he handed Elbert when he strolled past the Johnson's booth.

I tried to get myself together, but crap, it wasn't easy.

Billy Bob smiled at me. My stomach fluttered. Unfortunately, I hadn't noticed the pretty, blonde-haired woman directly behind him until she stepped into view. She moved up beside him and looped her arm around his. I wanted to punch her in her shiny, pretty face.

"Hey, doc," trilled Sunny. She waved at Billy Bob from across the room.

Thanks to Sunny and her haphazard psychic visions—and her penchant for finding trouble—she'd managed to lead the charge to find me before the hunters could finish me off. Sunny got to know the doc quite well during that time, and while she was married to my brother Babe, she and Billy Bob had maintained a close friendship. I couldn't be mad at her. She'd fought for my freedom, the way only a BFF can. She was beautiful inside and out, and I felt grateful to have her in my life. Today, she wore her golden hair in a ponytail. The style really showed off her large, striking green eyes. The pink V-neck shirt she'd just changed into showed off her other large assets as well. She'd already been blessed with good boobs before pregnancy. Now that she was nursing my adorable infant nephew, her boobs were almost in Dolly Parton territory.

The werewolf grinned at her. Hmph. Any idiot could see he was in love with my best friend. However, she was married to my brother, Babel, and Billy Bob making goo-goo eyes at her was plain ol' wrong. It had *nothing* to do with him not making goo-goo eyes at me.

"Hey, Sunny," he said back. "How you feeling?"

"Really good," she replied, all bright and perky. "Those herbs you gave me have really helped with Jude's colic."

He chuckled. "I'm glad to hear it. Bring him by next week for his five-month checkup."

"You got it." She smiled, her lashes batting hard enough to stir up a breeze.

"Anytime. You don't need an appointment." He laughed again. The sound hit all my buttons. I glared at Sunny. She noticed my look, smiled sweetly, and shrugged.

Apparently, I wasn't the only one glaring. The shiny little blonde, still clinging to Billy Bob's arm, shot daggers at my bestie. She clearly didn't want his attention focused anywhere else but on her. I tapped the counter to draw their attention away from Sunny. I'd hate to have to beat a bitch for making angry eyes at my friend.

She wasn't a local, which meant she was here for the festival. I wondered what her animal could be. Since I grew up an integrator, I'd never really learned all the characteristics for the different therian ethnicities. In their human forms, most therians had minor traits that revealed their inner animals. For example, werecoyotes have similar bone structure and build. We tend to be taller than average and have high cheekbones, wide mouths, square jaws, and straight noses. Raccoons, like Sheriff Taylor and his wife Jean, have the tale-tell darker circles around the eyes and wide cheeks. Ruth Thompson, one of my very good friends, and the local go-to gal is a spotted white tail deer. Deer are more delicate in their features, and they have the kind of beauty written about in fairy tales. They can seem almost nymph-like, even the men, like her husband Ed and all her boys.

Those were the obvious ones, but I'm unfamiliar with the therian groups outside of Peculiar, so I was no better than a human at identifying them. Of course, there are the hybrids as well, like Jo Jo, our bus boy-slash-waiter-slash-dishwasher who is half coyote, half mountain lion. His face is more narrow and longer than a normal coyote, but he has a similar height and build. Even still, if Ruth Thompson hadn't told me, I would never have guessed.

The blonde who clung to Billy Bob had a tiny nose and pouty lips and big, blue, doll eyes that all screamed weasel to me. Also, her itty bitty waist told me she wasn't drowning any sorrows in potato salad.

"Pie?" I asked her, pulling out a slice of coconut cream pie with coconut whipped topping from the refrigerated display case. I pushed it across the counter.

Her upper lip curled in disdain. At least, that's how I read it. She gazed pointedly at my mid-section then glanced down her svelte form.

"Why not," she said, pulling the pie across the counter. She picked up a fork from the silverware cups, scooped some pie up, and took a big bite. "Good." She sniffed, as if she'd had better, but was being polite. "I'm lucky," blondie said, taking another bite. "I can just eat and eat, and it never goes to my hips."

Oh, look, she shifts into a bitch. What a surprise.

I grabbed a pen and calculated the cost of the pie on a pad near the register. "That'll be $4.78."

Billy Bob pulled out his wallet. "It's on me, Chav. Bethany is the Arkansas *vulpes* representative on the council. I'm showing her around town today."

Vulpes meant she was a fox. And here I was hoping she was a werecow. But no, a fox! Could it get any more cliché? Ugh. And the way she fawned over Billy Bob, I swear if *Bethany* had been full of sunshine and rainbows they'd be shooting out of her eyeballs and her ass. She squeezed his arm harder and leaned closer to his body. "Thank you, William."

The pen in my hand snapped. William? William! Seriously? My temple throbbed with my quickening heartbeat. I couldn't believe she called him William. Nobody did that. I could see his own smile falter, but he turned up the charm. "You're welcome, Bethany."

So beguiling. So handsome. So frustrating! Ack! I snarled. The noise started in my chest and rumbled through my teeth and nose.

"Did you say something, Chav?" he asked. I swear I heard laughter in his voice.

I gritted my teeth. "Nope." I wanted to bite him and not in a sexy way.

He patted blondie's hand, the one permanently attached to his arm. He nodded to me. "Bethany will be leading the talks on therianthropic acclimation and normalization for new community members."

When I didn't respond, because a) I didn't care, and b) I didn't care, he added, "Bethany, this is Chavvah Trimmel. She used to be an integrator, but she's now a welcome addition to the town."

"Trimmel. Are you related to the mayor?" Bethany asked.

"He's my brother."

"Chavvah owns the restaurant with Sunny." Billy Bob gestured to Sunny.

"Sunny Trimmel," I said. "My sister-in-law. Married to the mayor. My brother." Just in case Billy Bob forgot she was married.

He smirked. "Chav and Sunny will be making all the vegetarian food for the banquet on Saturday night."

Great. I had been outed as an outsider and then relegated to mere caterer. "Did you want anything to go?" *So you can just go*, I mentally added.

"No," he said. "Just… Well, it doesn't matter." He waved his hand. "I'll see you around."

He turned on his heel, Bethany double-timing her steps to stay glued to his side. He didn't even stop to say bye to Sunny. Huh.

The lunch crowd dwindled, giving me space and time from Billy Bob's visit. I took pleasure in scrubbing the counters, as long as I didn't look too hard at the scars on my hands. Through some of the toughest times in my life, I've always been able to smile. My mother said I was a happy baby—the easiest of all her kids. I was the monkey in the middle between my two brothers, but since I was the only girl, it was easy to feel special. I used to be a happy person. Damn it. I am a happy person.

I *am* a happy person.

Staring at the spaces between my fingers, I let my hand go out of focus as I rubbed the counter in a circular motion. I forced my lips into a smile.

"Earth to Chav." Robbin Clubb, the local bookstore owner, was standing at the end of the counter with her wallet out. Next to her, Sharrall, her cousin, a were-mountain lion like Robbin, waited patiently for me to attend them.

Rushing over, I smiled and rang up her order. "Two hummus salad sandwiches with micro-greens and herbed soy cream cheese with two bags of home-fried sweet potato chips."

I was always surprised how many carnivores really loved our vegetarian food.

"Thanks, Chavvie," Sharrall said.

Robbin and Sharrall exited just as Ed Thompson, owner of Doe-Run Automotive and my friend Ruth's husband, walked in. He was a handsome man, even if a bit soft in the middle. I imagined Ruth's pies had a lot to do with the extra fluff. He had blond hair, the color of beach sand and dark brown eyes. They were wide and large, but not so much he looked like an alien. Typical for weredeer.

"Anywhere?" he asked, indicating a nearby booth.

"Sure, Ed."

Jo Jo was in a back booth, legs up on the bench, folding napkins and filling salt and pepper shakers. Our Jo Jo used to hang with a rowdy crowd, but over the last several years, he'd really matured into a responsible young man. I really didn't know what Sunny and I would do if it weren't for his help. Still, I wasn't sure if Ed would approve of the tattooed and pierced young man, especially since it appeared Jo Jo was dating Michele, one of Ed's older daughters.

I crossed the restaurant and smacked his size twelve combat boots hanging off the side of the padded bench. "Feet down, Jo Jo. You're on break, not at a day spa." I nodded to where Ed sat. "Besides, you got a customer."

My young friend scrambled up when he saw Ed and straightened his half-apron before walking over to take the deer-shifter's order.

Speaking of spas…oh, what I wouldn't have given at that moment to be at a day spa. There wasn't much I missed about living in California, but I did miss the pampering. I supposed we could drive to the city for a girl's day, but the restaurant required constant work. I looked at my bright red, shapely nails and had to admit, Dolly, who owned the local beauty shop, gave a mean manicure.

Mike Rogers, the owner of Grizzly Hardware, and yep, you guessed it, a bear shifter, walked in, his shoulders rounded forward, his mouth set in a grim line. He looked around for a second, spotted his target and headed straight for Ed. His dark brown hair was disheveled, and he held his meaty hands in tight fists.

Jo Jo yelped with surprise as Mike shoved him aside. I grabbed Jo Jo to stop him from getting involved then put myself between the nineteen-year-old and possible danger. My pulse sped up, and the voice I'd been hearing since my kidnapping, said, *Keep calm. You will not be harmed.*

The *voice* had kept me sane, kept me strong. It had been a coping mechanism according to Sunny and her pop psychology, a way to not be alone during the darkest hours of my life. Mike looked ready for a fight, and he'd probably triggered my imaginary friend. The voice seemed to pop up during times of extreme stress, pain, or fear. Right now, stress and fear were featuring prominently in my emotions. I was sure Ed could take care of himself, but I'd seen Mike lose his cool before.

At the town council meeting, he was one of the few people who wanted to tell the Tri-Council about Sunny being human. In fact, she was the only human in town, or at least, the only non-shifter. Since she was psychic, I didn't really know for sure if she was like a normal human. Since the baby, her gifts had been more miss than hit. Luckily, Mike had been voted down, but I didn't trust him not to blab. Babe and our town could be in a whole lot of trouble if the powers-that-be found out Sunny wasn't a therian. Damn it.

"You need to take this outside, Mike." I waved my hands. "Whatever this is."

"Ed here has recommended to the street vendors to get their hardware supplies at ACME in Lake Ozarks. He's been telling people I'm price gouging."

Ed didn't bother to stand up. "You've marked your prices up significantly this past week, Mike."

Mike's full cheeks puffed up red. "What business is it of yours?"

"I'm one of the town liaisons for the Tri-Council, and I told you two days ago that if you didn't lower your inflated prices, this would be the result."

"I won't have you tearing down my good name, Ed. I won't have you damaging my business reputation."

Ed turned his gaze up to Mike. "You've done that to yourself."

Mike tried to lunge for Ed, but I got between them, barely holding him off, and thankful he hadn't thrown a punch.

"Get out of here." I pushed harder against him, glad that Sunny had ducked into the kitchen. *This man is a coward. He will not act.* The voice in my head tried to reassure me, but I didn't want to take the chance. "Leave now before I call the sheriff."

Mike leaned in, his finger shaking as he pointed to Ed. "I'll see you rot for this, Ed Thompson. You haven't heard the last from me." He eased up, turned around, and walked out angrier than when he'd walked in.

"Holy crap."

"I'm sorry that happened here, Chav," Ed said.

"Me too," I told him. Fights in Sunny's Outlook were bad for business. Not to mention, my sanity. "Jo Jo, finish taking Ed's order."

You did well, sister.

Thanks, I told my imaginary friend. *Everything is good now. You can get out of my head.*

The dinner crowd hit hard about five-thirty. The omnivores and herbivores seemed to really like our Thursday specials of avocado and cucumber spring rolls and the roasted veggie wraps. The soup of the day was split pea, and the scent, thick and sweet, clung in the air. The soup made a great dipping sauce, too.

I'd be a happy-tired at closing time when I cashed out the drawers. Especially since the restaurant needed new drains and pipes. The old drains kept flooding, and it was a pain the ass to keep the sump pump running all the time—not to mention the extra cost on the electric bill as a result.

Yep, the Jubilee was good for business. The whole town felt a real sense of pride that Tri-State Council had decided to hold their annual mucky-muck celebration in Peculiar.

I glanced at Sunny, who'd just delivered an order to a table of four. There were times over the past couple of years when I had debated on whether I should bring her to Peculiar from California. I'll admit, seeing her and my younger brother Babe so happy made me simultaneously thrilled and nauseous at times, but I know I made the right call.

I really hoped she could get through the week without making waves with the visiting therians. The town might have accepted her as an official member of the community, but it didn't mean the outsiders would.

For now, I hoped we could keep Sunny's "humanness" a secret. The only way to truly tell a shifter was the see him or her shift. Sunny would need to stay hidden somewhere on the last day of the Jubilee when the full moon occurred—and every therian shifted whether they wanted to or not.

"Chavvie?" Jo Jo interrupted my train of thought. "Can I get off a little early tonight?"

"Got a hot date?"

"No." He blushed an amazing shade of pink. "It's just…well, I'd like to get a few groceries before I go home. Maybe show off my new mad cooking skills tonight."

His dad had been sober going on nine or ten months, but the kid was in a constant state of worry whether Brady would relapse. They lived on a property close to Judah's cabin where Sunny and Babe now lived. I'd taken over the tiny apartment above the restaurant. Sunny had made a good start of making it livable before she moved out. I'd gotten rid of all the old furniture and replaced it with a more coastal design or what Ruth liked to call modern beach rustic.

Jo Jo had stayed with me for a month while Brady had gotten sober. Now that he wasn't under my feet in the tiny apartment I called home, well, I missed the boy. I understood his fears about his dad, so I let him off the hook.

"Yeah, I can close by myself tonight." Sunny only worked token hours in the afternoon, now that she had a baby to take care of at home. But with Jo Jo gone, it was going to be a much longer night than I planned.

Jo Jo stood up, the top of his head nearly four inches above mine. He kissed my cheek. "Thanks, Chavvie. You're the best."

"Yeah, yeah," I told him. "Go peddle your charm where it might do you some good."

Ed Thompson finished the last sip of his coffee, put a dollar on the table, and limped to the cash register.

"Did you hurt yourself, Ed?" I asked as he counted exact change for his lunch.

"Just a catch in my step is all. Weather's gonna turn bad, I think."

It was the beginning of July, and the weather in Missouri fluctuated day to day, so I didn't have to be a psychic to predict it, I just knew change was inevitable. They had a saying in the state that went something like, "If you don't like the weather, stick around five minutes, it'll change."

"Do you think you could look at my car, Ed? It keeps making a clicking noise."

"Sure, Chav. Bring it on over anytime."

"If I get it to you tomorrow morning, when could you have it done?"

"Could be a timing problem. Unless it's something that I have to order parts for, no later than Friday."

"Sounds good."

Ed nodded, and with a wink and a smile, headed out. The doorbell jangled again, three men walked in. The first man had short brown hair, about two weeks overdue for a haircut, so it curled over his ears. He was tall, well built, and his green eyes shined like peridots framed by thick dark lashes. The second of the men was thin and wiry, nice-looking in his own way, with blue eyes, red hair, and freckles. The third, a dark blond with brown eyes was built like an Olympic swimmer with a broad chest, narrow hips, and long, muscular arms. All three came to the register.

"Can I get you gentlemen a table?" I asked.

"No," said the man with pale green eyes. "We need some sandwiches and coffee to go."

"Cream and sugar?"

The redhead piped up. "Yes, for me."

"Only sugar," the dark blond said.

"I'll take mine black," the green-eyed man said.

"And what sandwiches?" I pulled out my order pad and held up a pen, ready to write.

"Jackfruit burger with jalapeños."

"Your California roll with extra avocado."

"I'll take the roasted red pepper panini with cream cheese."

"Chips and a dill pickle spear all around?"

Each man nodded. They stood off to the side. I asked Jo Jo get the coffees, and I went back to the kitchen to make the sandwiches. Ten minutes later, I carried the order, wrapped and ready to go to the register.

The dark blond with the brown eyes leaned close. "Mmm. Those smell good."

I put the sandwiches into a bag, added three servings of homemade potato chips and three baggies with a dill pickle spear each, napkins, and plastic silverware. Jo Jo arrived with three coffee to-go cups.

"Anything else?" I asked.

"Your name," the blond said.

I looked up, startled by the question. He had the hint of a smile on his wide mouth, and I noticed tiny gold flecks in his brown eyes that almost glittered like...well, glitter.

"Chavvah," I said. "Are you all with the council or just in early for the Jubilee?"

Brown eyes made some very direct eye contact, and his smile grew wider. "I'm Randy Lowry. My father is the head of the council. I'm just a humble handyman." He pointed to the redhead. "That's Hans Fisk. Council member representing the big cats of Arkansas." He jerked his thumb at the good-looking guy with pale green eyes. "And that guy is Dominic Tartan. He's a friend of Thomas Decker, one of the Missouri Reps."

Dominic stepped up and held out his hand. "Enough about us," he said when I gave his hand a shake. "I'd like to know more about you. Like when do you get off work?"

I laughed. I couldn't help myself. One, he was very cute. And two, I'd spent the last eight months with people seeing me as damaged goods. It was really nice to have a man look at me like a woman and not a victim. "Considering I own the place, not until it closes."

"I'd love to have a drink or something if you're interested."

"Tartan!" Randy Lowry said grinning. "Dude. You stole my thunder."

Dominic laughed, and I liked the ease of him. "Snooze, you lose, Lowry." He winked at me.

I shook my head and smiled. "Not tonight. I'm beat." I took pleasure in his disappointment. God, how I wished Billy Bob were in the restaurant now! Oh, my God. I did *not* just think that. Ack! "But I'll be available Sunday afternoon if you'd like to get a bite to eat down at Blonde Bear Café?"

Dominic grinned. "It's a date, Chavvah."

I cast a coy glance his way as he turned to leave. "Looking forward to it," I said softly. He stopped, turned back, and smiled.

"I have a date," I said out loud after they left. Suddenly, my stomach felt squidgy, and I resisted the urge to run after Dominic and cancel.

After seven, the place was nearly empty. I walked to Sunny, who'd put her feet up in one of the booths. I put my hands on her shoulders and rubbed. "Why don't you go home, hon? It's been a long day, and I don't expect them to get any shorter this week. I'll finish cleaning up."

She reached across her large, ballooning breasts and patted my hand. "I suppose you're right. Besides, I need to get home and empty these suckers before they explode." She gave me a wry look. "Again." She sighed. "I should have pumped before the dinner crowd, but we've just been too busy." She handed me a wad of bills from her half-apron. "Some really great tips today." She put her finger to her temple as if she were getting a vision. "I see new drains in our future."

"Woo hoo." I knew her visions had been scarce since giving birth to Jude. I think it bothered her more than she let on. "If you say it, it must be true."

"You don't have to say that." She grabbed her boobs with both hands. "Noooo," she whined.

I looked at her chest, it was hard not to, and damn, and the front of her pink top was soaked. "You're leaking all over the place. You need to start wearing nursing pads or something." She complained they gave her saucer-nipples.

She crossed her arms over her breast, making the milk flow harder. "I think that's my cue to leave."

I smiled. "Do you want me to call Babe to come get you?" The door jangled again, and my brother sauntered in as if on cue. "Speak of the devil."

"Hey, baby," Sunny said, more tired and worn out than a few seconds ago.

I realized she'd been trying to be chipper for our customers, for me even, but with Babe here she could let her guard completely down. She didn't have to pretend. I glanced at my scars. One of these days, maybe I could stop pretending.

My brother was tall and built like a boxer. He'd slicked back his normally shaggy, brown hair and wore a blue, button-down dress shirt under his leather jacket, and a new pair of black slacks. As mayor, he'd been in charge of getting the Tri-Council meeting organized, and he looked nearly as worn out as Sunny.

"Damn, you look rode hard and put away wet, Babe."

"Not yet," Sunny quipped, followed by a giggle. Babel's haggard expression changed instantly to a leering grin.

Ew. I chose to ignore them.

"Hey, Chav." He leaned down and kissed my cheek, but his eyes never left Sunny. "Aww, darling. You're having a rough go." He held his hand out to her. "You ready to go home?"

Sunny scooted to the edge of the booth and turned her swollen feet out.

"Damn." Babel winced. "It's time I got you off those turnips." He scooped her into his arms. Sunny laughed as he spun her once. He didn't seem to mind that his shirt got wet from her boob leakage.

"Get on out of here, you two." I shooed them toward the door. "I'll see you all tomorrow."

When eight o'clock rolled around, I was happy to see the last of our customers leave. I took my apron off, hung it on a hook just inside the kitchen door, and sat down to put my feet up. I'd already cleaned the grill. All I had left to do was give everything a good wipe down, sweep and mop the floors, and clean the toilets in our universal bathroom. I checked it every hour during the day, so I knew it wouldn't be too bad.

I wished I wasn't so tired. Since my injuries had been so substantial (Billy Bob's words), I didn't have the same energy I'd had pre-kidnapping. The only time I felt any kind of normalcy was after a full moon shift, but my upbringing as an integrator made it difficult for me to give over to my animal side. The advantage to living in a therian community is that I didn't have to hide my second nature, but I couldn't bring myself to let my coyote flag fly.

I put in my ear buds and plugged in an audiobook. Listening to stories let me travel to other places while I did my chores. Really, it had become my favorite part of the day. Forty minutes later, or thereabout, I put away the mop, cleaned out the bucket, and turned off the book. I turned the lights off from inside the kitchen where a master switch controlled everything but the refrigerated units. My bed was calling me hard, and I considered waiting until morning to shower.

Since my apartment was over the restaurant, it would take me ten seconds to get home and on my way to bed. But first, I had to take out the garbage to the bin outside. We kept a Dumpster at the back of the restaurant as far from the backdoor as possible. I didn't bother turning on the lights again since I knew the path by heart. As I carried two large bags of stinky trash to the large bin, I fantasized about my fluffy mattress and my bamboo pillow.

The next thing I knew I was airborne, the garbage bags flying in different directions. I managed to twist, landing on my shoulder and hip.

What the hell?

I rolled to a sitting position and leaned forward, trying to see what I had tripped over. My palms slid around in a wet, sticky puddle. I noticed my shirt was soaked, and now that the shock wore off, I could smell the metallic tinge of blood and something else. Sweet like root beer, only spicier. I scrabbled backward, heart racing. I popped to my feet, returned to the kitchen, and turned on the outside lights.

Less than a foot from the back door laid a human-like body. It had no hair. No skin. No face. Its hollowed sockets stared blindly upward, and its mouth gaped wide, revealing straight, even teeth. My stomach roiled with nausea as I viewed the meaty red corpse.

Blood soaked the ground, offering a terrifying backdrop for a horrific display of what had once been a person.

They found me. The hunters. A warning about—no. No. They were dead. Each and every one of them. Dead, dead.

Your enemies are no more, little sister.

I took immediate comfort from the imaginary voice, and my panic subsided.

I scrambled into the kitchen, shutting and locking the door behind me. I tried to slow down my heaving breaths and calm my pounding pulse.

You are safe.

What a messed up lie, I thought. I wasn't safe. I'm not sure I'd ever been. But the voice once again helped me to clear my jumbled thoughts. I dug my cell phone out of the back pocket of my jeans, tapped it open, and dialed the Sheriff's office.

"Deputy Farraday," a man said. "How can I help you?"

"Eldin," I said, my voice shaking. "This is Chavvah. You need to wake up the sheriff."

CHAPTER 2

"AND YOU TURNED OFF the light and walked out here and tripped over the body?" Sheriff Taylor asked for the millionth time. The dark circles under his eyes made him look as tired as I felt. His appearance had more to do with the fact that his second nature was a raccoon. Mine was actual exhaustion. The sheriff stood over the body, and I leaned against the doorjamb. Deputy Farraday had been taking pictures and making notes. The town coroner and local funeral director, Mark Smart, prepared a body bag.

Why would someone leave a freshly skinned corpse outside a vegetarian restaurant? Was it a statement from some crazy meat eaters?

I didn't want to think about the question hovering just outside my potential hysteria. *Was this poor soul someone I knew?*

"Chavvah?"

"Yes," I finally responded. "That's what happened." I felt sick to my stomach, and now that the adrenaline had completely worn off, I could smell every sickly, rancid bit of the man's exposed muscle and fat. I averted my gaze from the ghastly sight, but my other shifter senses were on high alert. I didn't think I'd ever be able to get that particular stench out of my nose.

"You didn't hear anything?"

"Like I said, I had my ear buds in, listening to a book." I put my hand on my belly to stop a wave of queasiness. "I can't believe…" My breath quickened, and I swallowed the rising bile. "…this happened."

Sheriff Taylor joined me near the back door and squeezed my shoulder. "I'm real sorry, Chav."

I saw movement around the corner, and my heart jumped into my throat. I grabbed the sheriff's shoulder, but then I recognized the silver glint of Billy Bob's hair. *Shit.* The doc was the last person I wanted seeing me covered in blood and looking, once again, like a victim.

The werewolf strode directly to us, barely glancing at the body. His stare was intense as his gaze pinned mine. "Are you okay?" The low, throaty growl that followed the question sent shivers down my skin.

I nodded, worried that if I opened my mouth, I'd start crying.

Billy Bob turned to the sheriff. "Do you know who it is?"

"No. Mark's pretty certain it's a man, even with his skin and genitals removed." He winced as he spoke.

"We can't figure out if it's one of ours or one of the people who came in for the Jubilee." I could hear a sad weariness in his tone. Our town had already been through so much, and this murder compounded the misery with interest. "Doc, you'll have to help us ID the victim."

As the only medical doctor for miles around, and really, the only one qualified to examine a therian body, Billy Bob would do the autopsy. Call me a chicken, but I couldn't stay there within three feet of a skinned corpse and talk about it—him. "I ... I think I'll go shower now."

"I know you want to clean up, Chav," the sheriff said. "But you did the right thing in waiting until we arrived." He snapped his fingers at Farraday, who trotted over with a paper bag. "I need you to put all your clothes in this bag after you change. Also, I don't think you should stay here tonight. Why don't you stay with Sunny and Babe for a few days?"

Sunny and Babel were having enough issues with Baby Jude not sleeping through the night. They were both exhausted, and I didn't want to upset Sunny. Not tonight. Besides, I couldn't deal with my friend's reaction to blood. Sunny was notoriously squeamish and tended to faint.

"Chavvah can stay with me," said Billy Bob.

"Uh, no." I racked my brain for alternatives. I didn't want to go to Billy Bob's place. One, it was attached to his clinic, and I still had a lot of painful memories of my recovery, and two, I couldn't stand the idea of sleeping just feet away from Billy Bob, knowing he'd never see me as anything more than a patient. "I'll go to Ruth's."

"It's after ten, Chavvah." He used his doctor tone—the one that suffered no arguments. "There's no sense in waking her and Ed this late at night."

"Besides, they took in two of the Jubilee attendees," added the sheriff. "They've already got tight quarters."

Desperate, I seized on a ridiculous thought. "I'll sleep at the motel."

The Halliver's Hilltop Motel was a thirty-bed unit just outside of town on the same rural road that led to Sunny and Babel's cabin. Homer and Audrey Halliver, a nice young were-raccoon couple, managed the motel.

Billy Bob lifted an eyebrow. "The rooms are booked. But maybe Bethany could let you share her room at the Halliver's."

The knowing look in his eyes made me want to punch him in his perfectly flawless kissable kisser. Billy Bob or Bitch?

I took the lesser of two evils.

"Fine," I said, making sure he heard the irritation in my acquiescence. I snatched up the paper bag for my bloody clothes. "I'll be right back."

* * * *

Blood colored the shower stall.

As the hot water poured over me, the memory of getting clean after sitting in my own filth and blood for three weeks rolled back on me like a dust devil on a hot highway. My imaginary friend began to chant. I couldn't understand the words bouncing in my mind, but I understood the soothing tone. Calmness stole my panic, and I released a pent-up breath.

It took all of about fifteen minutes to shower, change my clothes and pack an overnight case. I didn't want to stay longer than a day or two. When I got back downstairs, I found Billy Bob and the sheriff in the kitchen. The back door was still open. One glance out the back door confirmed that the body had been removed. But the blood-soaked dirt remained. A terrible reminder of the carnage.

Crap. Jo Jo was supposed to open in the morning to prep the food. Over the past year, he'd become a very competent sous-chef. I made a mental note to set my phone alarm so I could call him in the a.m. before he came to work.

Silently, I handed the paper bag to the sheriff. Billy Bob stared at my overnight case and frowned.

"You got enough for a few days?" Billy Bob's low baritone voice sent a shiver through my belly to my girly parts.

Oh, Lord, going to spend the night at his place was such a bad idea. "I have everything I need for a short stay." *A very, very short stay.* "Sheriff, do you want me for anything else?"

"Come down to the station in the morning and fill out a witness statement. You two can go." The sheriff cast a furtive glance at Billy Bob then me.

"Am I missing something?" I asked, suspicious. What was this all about?

"No, ma'am," Sheriff Taylor said. "You all have a safe drive," he added.

My left shoulder ached, the one that had been ripped from its socket and left to mend out of place. My body held too many reminders of being tortured by my kidnappers. I switched the small suitcase to the right hand. Billy Bob reached out for it, but I stopped him. "I'm not an invalid."

His brow wrinkled with irritation, but suddenly, his gaze landed on mine, and his face softened. He nodded. "Let's get going then."

* * * *

The ride in his half-ton truck was like sitting in a Jon boat as it crossed a choppy wake. "Jesus, Doc. You ever heard of shocks?"

"This beauty is reliable." He patted his dashboard, his gray eyes shining as moonlight streamed into the cab. "I can count on it to get me where I'm going."

"Yes, but can you count on it to get you there free of hemorrhoids?"

He smiled, and my pulse quickened. It made me stupidly happy to see the corners of his lips tug up. "I heal fast."

I laughed, the repulsive image of the skinned corpse fading with each minute in Billy Bob's presence. "You'd have to."

He chuckled. My lady bits clenched. Ugh.

"How have you been?" he asked.

His concern flattened my woo-woo feelings, and my lady bits unclenched. "Fine." My throat was tight. "Are you going to do the autopsy on the body?"

"Yes," he said. "Mark Smart will transport the victim to the clinic."

"Tonight?" I hadn't thought about where or when Billy Bob would examine the body, but when he'd asked me to stay at his house, I'd just assumed it would happen tomorrow.

"I need to identify him." He shook his head, his eyes tight at the corners. "For his family. It's not fair to let him go unclaimed by his people."

My stomach hurt. For too long, my younger brother Judah and the other victims of those insidious hunters had gone unclaimed. I remember what it had been like for the two years before we discovered why my brother had disappeared. I'd never stopped wondering or worrying. My emotions had run the rainbow of anger to grief to hope to denial and back to anger. I didn't want another family to suffer the same experience. Not even for a day.

I nodded sharply. "Good." I swallowed. The heat of anxious energy burned in my gut.

Billy Bob put on his blinker before turning up his long driveway. We passed his sweat lodge. I couldn't buy into all his shaman bullshit. Yes, we had the ability to transform into animals, but that didn't mean every type of magical crap out there was real. When we crested the hilltop, his house appeared. It was a large, one-level ranch home with the clinic attached on the nearest side.

The outside lights were on, illuminating the large front porch that stretched the length of the house, maybe sixty feet long and eight feet wide. The place had two front doors about twenty feet apart. One was Billy Bob's private entrance to his home, and the other was the public door to the clinic. A van was parked near the clinic door, the lights off.

Billy Bob turned the truck off. "Smart is here with the…" He looked at me.

I swallowed the knot in my throat. "Do you need help?"

His expression flashed with surprise. "Are you sure you want to help?"

What he was really asking was, *Can you handle it?* I nodded, telling myself to woman up. "I'm tough, Doc."

"That you are." He put his hand on my forearm and gave it a squeeze.

His touch electrified my skin with an energy that pulsed through my body. I pulled away from him as if I'd touched a hot coal. He thinned his lips, his gaze now on the steering wheel.

- 35 -

"We better get to it," I said to cover my embarrassment. Shit. What was wrong with me?

I should have apologized. He was being kind. It wasn't his fault my stupid hormones did a jig every time he walked into a room, or that my whole being wanted him whenever he touched me. It was as if he was the socket and I was the bulb. Every time he touched me my body would light up. I'd never had that reaction to another man. Ever. I'd like to say it was some transference because he was my doctor, my caregiver, during some of my darkest hours, but truthfully, he'd made me feel that way before I'd been kidnapped.

He opened his door, got out, and shut it hard behind him. I winced. After a few calming breaths, I got out too. By the time I reached the clinic, Billy Bob and Mark had already pulled the victim out of the back of the funeral home van on a gurney. Billy Bob handed the key to Mark's oldest son, Jackson, who had gone into business with his father right out of high school.

I caught up with Jackson at the door. His face looked as pale as his pale blond, almost white hair, typical of opossum shifters. "You okay?" I asked.

"I never saw anything like that, Chav." He shook his head, his eyes haunted.

I could smell vomit on his breath. Poor guy must have gotten sick. I'd lived in a cage for almost three weeks with only a bucket for my bodily functions, and sometimes, they'd messed me up so badly I couldn't use it. Even so, seeing that skinned corpse, having its blood cover me, had almost made me empty my stomach too.

I patted his shoulder and took the keys from his shaking hands. "Why don't you go sit on one of those benches? Get some fresh air."

He didn't argue with me. Shoulders slumped, he walked the ten feet to the nearest bench and sat down. Billy Bob and Mark had pulled the gurney up the ramp by the time I got there to help. I put the door wedge in to hold it open so I could get out of their way and then followed them inside.

"You have anyone in the clinic tonight, Dr. Smith?" Mark asked.

"No," he said. "Nothing too major this week to warrant an overnight stay. I guess I can be grateful for that."

I was grateful I wasn't the body being moved to the metal table in his surgical suite. After all, the body had been left near my restaurant…while I was in the kitchen. Suddenly the air left my lungs as if I'd been socked in the stomach. "I was there," I said.

"What, Chavvah?" Billy Bob asked.

I looked at him, and I could feel the blood drain from my face. "I was cleaning the kitchen." My hand went to my trembling lips. "The killer was right outside the door. He could have waited until I … Damn it, Doc. He could have killed me too."

Strong arms wrapped around me before I realized that Billy Bob had me in his embrace. I could hear his heart thumping as I pressed my face against his chest. I'm tall, only an inch shy of six foot, but next to Billy

Bob most people were short. His hands threaded my hair, still damp from the shower, and my skin pulsed, threatening to strip my self-control. I wanted to shift. To run. To forget about my human side. My broken, damaged, emotionally stunted human side, and just let instinct and nature take over.

"You smell like the woods and the wind," Billy Bob whispered to me. "You smell of home."

I pulled back, curiously freaked out. What game was he playing? "I need some air." I stepped out of his arms. "I'll be back in a few minutes."

"Why don't you just go on over to the house," he said. "After the Smarts get on their way, I'll show you the guest room. Until then, get something to eat or drink from the kitchen." He raised a brow. "There's a liquor cabinet in the living room if you want something stronger than water or tea."

"Thanks," I told him and meant it. "You have bourbon."

He smiled. "Yep."

"Awesome." I headed out the door of the surgical suite without a single look back. I wanted to lose myself in a glass of liquid amber.

I'd never been in Billy Bob's home before, the non-medical side of his ranch house, so, I really hadn't known what to expect. Maybe something rustic, a lot of weathered wood, and oh, I don't know, dream catchers. Something in the Southwestern motif of design. It was none of that. The walls were pale green but earthy and warm with brown and gold accents. The furniture was modern, but still comfortable and inviting. The living room had a large fireplace, a deep brown semi-circular sofa with a round coffee table made of several types of wood that complimented the rest of the room. On the wall nearest me, I saw a tall liquor cabinet with see-through doors. The alcohol bottles were neatly shelved by type.

I retrieved a highball glass from the lower part of the cabinet where I also spotted a built-in ice maker. Fancy. I plopped a couple of chunks into my glass and grabbed the only bottle of bourbon in the cabinet. I took a long pull straight from the bottle. The potent liquor burned its way down my throat to my stomach. I waited for the blossoming warmth I knew would come. When it finally did, I poured two fingers into the glass and made my way to the sofa. It was July, so there was no need for a fire in the fireplace, but still, I huddled around my glass of booze as if it were ablaze.

I could smell Billy Bob's scent—earthy musk with a hint of bergamot permeating everything in the room, including my shirt, which had been pressed up against him. Sometimes a heightened sense of smell could be a curse. At least the scent of the freshly murdered man was gone. I reclined against the backrest of the couch, marveling at the comfort, when I heard the door between his clinic and home open, his footsteps down the hallway, his slow, steady breathing as he entered the room.

"Hey, Doc," I said, without turning around to look at him.

"Hey," he said back. "I see you found the bourbon."

I held up my glass and shook it so the ice clinked. "Yep." I sighed and closed my eyes. "It's nice."

"If you're ready, I'll give you a quick tour and take you to your room."

I stood up and turned my gaze on him. He was carrying my overnight bag. "Oh, shoot. Thanks." I strolled to him and tried to take it, but he waved me off.

"I'll take it. No, argument, please."

"I'm too tired to argue anyhow." I wanted to forget about the night, but I knew some things would be burned into my memories no matter how much brain bleach I applied.

I let him lead the way down a wide, wainscoted hallway, and couldn't stop myself noticing the nice view aka his firmly, muscular ass in some spectacular fitted jeans. Jesus, why was I thinking about his butt? There was a dead man in the clinic next door, possibly a neighbor, even a friend, and here I was letting my hormones have their way. I felt like the most awful human being ever.

He slowed up, and his scent grew stronger, the bergamot turning bright and citrusy to my senses. He stopped at a door near the end of the hall. I crossed my arms because my stupid nipples had gone rigid with alert. He put down the case and pivoted to face me. The raw expression in his silvery-gray eyes melted me to my toes. I gulped.

- 40 -

"Uh, this my room?"

"Yes," he said.

"Where is your room?"

His eyes darkened with an expression I hadn't seen before. "Right across the hall." He reached back and rapped the knuckles of his left hand on the door.

"Oh. That close."

"Don't worry," he growled in a very un-Billy Bob way. "I won't bother you tonight."

"I didn't…" I realized I didn't know how to respond.

"If you need me I'll be in the clinic."

"Right," I said. "Right. The guy."

He pointed at the door just up the hall from the guest bedroom. "Bathroom if you need it." His words were tight, squeezed, as if his throat had swelled. He didn't open the door for me. Instead, he skirted around me as if I had Ebola and quickly walked away down the hall and out of sight.

What the hell was that all about? I'd never seen Billy Bob act so strangely. It had to be the body. Had he found something? Something that affected him personally? Or me? "Oh God." I put my hand to my mouth. What if it really was someone I knew? Someone close to me? I hadn't looked close enough to determine the height or build of the corpse. I'd wanted so badly to get away from it. I couldn't even put a voice to my worst fears. I wouldn't. I'd already lost one brother.

My hands shook bad enough that I dropped the highball glass. It didn't shatter but ice skid across the hardwood floor and bourbon splattered everywhere. I sprinted up the hall, my wet soles sliding as I tried to slow down for the transition around the corner. I slammed to the floor, landing hard on my backside. The impact made my right leg throb with renewed pain, and my elbow bleed where it had smacked into wainscoting trim. It made me angry that I couldn't keep the tears from my eyes as I pulled myself up from the floor and limped down the next hall toward the clinic.

CHAPTER 3

I COULDN'T CALM MY racing pulse or my ragged breathing as I burst through the door. The stench of death overwhelmed me for a second. It was sweet, I noted, almost gamey, like the way rabbit meat smelled.

Billy Bob stepped out of the surgical room. I must have been a hot mess because his eyes widened with alarm. "What's happened? Is someone in the house? You're bleeding." He stripped the surgical gloves from his hands and rushed to me, his speed dizzyingly fast. He grasped my upper arms, his face a mixture of panic and rage. His voice grew unnaturally low. "Who hurt you? I will kill him!"

His aura, which is the only way I could think to describe what I felt, surrounded me, heady and heavy, until I thought I would pass out. "I'm...No one," I finally said. "The body. I just...Is it..." When he wrapped me in his arms again. I didn't fight him. I let the heat of his comfort seep into my skin.

"No, Chavvah," he murmured softly. "No. It's not Babe. It's not your brother."

I let the tears fall as relief flooded me. Still, I was sickened. This was someone's brother, husband, son... someone loved the person on the table as much as I loved Babe, and they would soon grieve in a way that no one ever expects when the life of a loved one is ripped away from them under such violent and evil circumstances.

When I finally calmed myself enough to speak, and sadly, had smeared my snot across Billy Bob's chest, I asked, "Do you know who it is?"

My stomach dropped at his solemn expression. "No," he said, his voice so quiet I could barely hear him. "But it might be Ed."

"What?" I shook my head. "Ed Thompson?" He'd just been in for lunch today. He was fine. Right as rain. I couldn't be Ed. Not Ed.

Billy Bob nodded.

"Oh." My hand went to my mouth. "Ruth. Oh no. Who is going to tell Ruth?"

* * * *

I sneezed. Twice. The feather top guest bed was comfortable, but my allergies to goose down along with my fears for Ed, knowing he was killed just outside the back door, and I hadn't even noticed. I'd been in my own bubble for what? Forty minutes? That wasn't enough time to remove the skin from a fresh corpse.

No. He had most likely been skinned somewhere else and brought to the dump site.

My skin itched and my fingers lingered over a deeper more substantial scar on my forearm. I recalled the injury with terrible clarity…

"Stubborn bitch," one of my captors said. He had brown hair and blue eyes, and he smelled like wintergreen chewing tobacco. I pulled against the restraints, but three days without water had left me dehydrated and weak. "All you have to do is change into the animal you are, and this will end."

The other man, a middle-aged blond, held his phone up and recorded us.

Wintergreen waved a chisel, one used for woodwork, in front of my face. He held the angled tip against my forearm. "Last chance," he said.

I closed my eyes.

The sharp sound of the hammer as it struck the metal chisel rang out against the aluminum walls of the Morton building.

Noise, small and pathetic, snapped me from the memory. I realized it had come from me. A whimper. Better than the screams I could still hear when I thought of that torturous night. That's when I noticed the tall shadow inside the room by the closed door.

I scrambled to sit up, rolling off the bed on the far side to put distance between the intruder and me. I summoned my animal, using my coyote eyes to scan the room and get a better look. I saw the painting of the rolling Ozark hills, the eight-drawer dresser, a tall bookshelf, a closed closet door, and the very bright moonlight streaming in from the window.

No intruder.

I scented the air, but I couldn't detect anything foreign. Besides, what kind of idiot would intrude on a werewolf's territory? Billy Bob wouldn't allow it.

"You've suffered much, little wolf," a familiar voice said. My friendly neighborhood imaginary buddy ... except he was more like an actual presence than a pesky voice in my head.

"I'm losing my mind," I muttered.

"I would not choose someone feeble-minded," said an offended male voice.

Not in my head.

In the room.

Movement near the door startled me. I crouched low, my hands up, ready to attack. "Who are you?" A gravelly rumble built in my chest. No way I'd be taken again. Not this time. Not ever again.

"I am known by many names, sister. *Pia'isa*, *kweo kachina*, and *mai-coh* to name a few."

"Well, your new name will be mud if Doctor Smith, the owner of this house, finds you. He'll rip you a new asshole."

He wasn't a town resident, which meant he had to be one of the men who'd come in for the Jubilee. His face was shadowed. Even with my coyote-vision, I couldn't make out his features. I tried to hone in on other appearance landmarks. He was well over six and a half feet tall. His shoulders were as wide if not wider than Billy Bob's. His language was stiff and stilted as if every word cost him something. Finally, and most oddly, it felt as if his breath stirred the air around me. But the weirdest thing of all was the sense of calm that overrode my stirring panic.

"What do you want?"

"Ah." The dark figure shook his head. "There is no need to fear me. I mean you no harm, little wolf." I felt another wave of calm. "You know me. We often speak, sister."

The voice in my head sometimes called me sister, and the awareness jolted me. At some point when my imaginary pal first started talking to me, I'd convinced myself it had been Judah, my older brother, the one who'd been killed.

"I'm a coyote," I said. *Because that's soooo important.* "A therian, not a lycan."

"You are wolf, child. That above all else."

The denial died on my lips. Recently I'd found out that my grandmother had been half-lycanthrope, but as a werecoyote, I'd grown up despising werewolves. My brothers and I had been taught that lycanthropes were dangerous and unpredictable. A rogue pack had killed both my grandparents before I was born, which only strengthened my family's views about the species. So, I had no intention of claiming the heritage, let alone giving it precedence over my coyote blood.

I'd backed up to the window, my fingers on the frame. I had no doubt the huge, hulking figure between me and the door could take my head off. My claws bit into my flesh as my fingers began to shift. I needed to hold it together. Keep the element of surprise to myself.

"You don't need to run from me, sister. I am not your enemy."

"A friend doesn't sneak into your bedroom," I said.

"I do not sneak," he said. Again, his tone reflected offense.

Noise in the hallway had him turning his head away from me. I used the opportunity to throw myself backward through the window. I cried out when the broken glass bit into my back as I landed on the grassy lawn, but I didn't wait for the weird dude to chase me. I didn't know what scared me more, that he claimed ownership of my imaginary friend or that I wasn't nearly as frightened as I should've been.

Who cares? Run, you moron.

I shucked my nightgown and my underwear, finding freedom as my body mid-run began to change. My bones moved and reformed, fur sprouted down out of my skin with a whispering tingle that the full shift to animal form always brought on. It was pleasure, not pain, and it was why my family always warned against changing when it wasn't necessary. During the first night of the full moon, the shift came without being called, and unfortunately, therians become true animals on those nights. Acting on pure instinct alone. It was dangerous for everyone around, humans and shifters alike. But when therians chose to change at any other time, they could think and remember as if they were still in human form. It made the impulse to stay a beast strong, the feeling of being in animal form while able to keep clear headed, intoxicating. I tried not to think of the joy. It would distract me and get me kidnapped again, or worse, killed.

A howl in the distance startled me. On four legs now, my senses heightened, I ran in a full out sprint toward the woods behind Billy Bob's house. I caught a fading scent of a wolf on one of the trails and the faint aroma of bergamot. Billy Bob. Of course, he ran these woods in his lycan form. I had been born and raised in Kansas City, and I'd never been much of a country girl, not until these past couple of years, but even then, I hadn't done much exploring. Would it be safer to follow where Billy Bob had roamed, or try to make my own way deep into the Ozarks?

Another howl drove my choice. I took off through thickets of briars and stick'ems, past oaks, maples, and evergreens. A fallen tree just up ahead of me had to be four feet thick in diameter and gray with age and decay. I leaped with all my might to get over the top. The wind ruffled my fur, my belly scraping against the dry bark as I dove head first into a shallow creek on the other side. I yelped then inhaled the water, the cold liquid soaking me to the skin. I stood up and shook, droplets spraying everywhere. The running stream chilled the pads of my paws.

I sloshed toward the far bank, only twenty feet away, the stream rising until my paws could no longer touch. I paddled hard, keeping my nose above the water.

"Chavvah!"

The sound of my name brought me up short. I glanced back, and my head went under as I saw a very naked Billy Bob standing on this side of the log. I turned back toward the other side of the creek bed and kept going until I was able to get on dry ground on the opposite side. We'd had plenty of rain this month and fighting the current had taken it out of me.

I panted, trying to gather my wits. Had the wolf howls come from Billy Bob and not the intruder? In my panic, had I been running from him the whole time? I felt like an idiot. A fool. *A scared foolish idiot.* I stared at Billy Bob, the moonlight dancing on his flawless skin, the shadows enhancing every cut of his muscles. He didn't make a move toward me as if he knew I would rabbit if spooked. He simply waited, his brow furrowed with concern.

Finally, I shook out my fur again, allowing the shift back to my human form. When the change completed, I was crouched low on the ground still staring at the doc.

"Are you okay?" he asked when my heavy breathing died down.

"There was a man in your home," I said. "In my room." God, what if it had been the killer? Had he followed me from town?

His eyes widened. He pursed his lips. "Are you hurt?"

The glass in my back stung suddenly as if to remind me that I'd thrown myself out of a window. I turned so he could see my back and said, "I'll live." I hadn't felt it in my coyote form. "How did he get inside, Doc? How did he find me?"

"You're safe now," he said. "If someone were near, I'd smell him. It's just you and me now." His voice was low and soothing.

I plopped back onto my ass. I appreciated that he didn't ask me if I'd had a bad dream or try to tell me I was overwrought. Now that I was away from the intruder, the strange Zen I'd experienced had evaporated under a cold dose of fear. The sharp rocks from the shore dug into my skin. I ignored the pain. I'd had worse. I hugged my knees, burying my face in the crack between them. I'd never forget the man. His presence had been weighted. Undeniable.

"Do you want to come over here?"

"No," I told him.

"Do you want me to come over there?"

I remained silent and let him interpret my lack of response how he wanted. The water sloshed and a small sense of satisfaction slid through me. I lifted my head and peeked. Billy Bob was nearly waist deep in the creek and half way across. As the water level lowered, I got a really great shot of his package, and... "Wow." Let's just say that the cold water had very little effect on him.

He stopped just shy of the shore. "What?"

"What?" Crap, I'd said, "Wow," out loud. He really was gorgeous. His skin was a perfect shade of heavily creamed coffee and completely unblemished. Unlike my own, which was scarred and knotted in multiple places. I suddenly wished he hadn't crossed. Self-consciously, I hugged my knees harder to hide my ravaged skin.

"Chavvah," he said.

I looked up at him, reluctantly meeting his gaze.

"Is it so difficult to look at me?" He held his hands out to his side. "Do you really dislike me so much?"

I didn't want him to know how much I cared. How much my feelings had grown for him since my rescue. He was the only one who hadn't made me feel all victim-y and TSTL, too stupid to live. But he'd always been strictly professional with me, and I knew how much he liked, maybe even loved, Sunny. I wouldn't be second best, not for any man. I wanted someone who wanted me above all others.

"I don't dislike you."

"Then stop pushing me away." He walked the rest of the way over and sat down on the rocks next to me. I tried really hard not to stare at his dangly parts. "Turn so I can see your back."

I did. He grasped my shoulder with his left hand, and with his right, he plucked the larger shards of window glass from my flesh. I didn't flinch. I didn't even whimper at the pain. Instead, I rubbed the gnarled scar at my elbow and let my mind go elsewhere.

"Tell me about the intruder?"

I shivered. "He was large, larger than you even." I shook my head. "His face was hidden in shadow, his whole body really. I could make out his shape, but not any features."

"Did he say anything?"

I snorted. "Yeah. He was really chatty for a psychopath."

"Like?" He pulled out another piece of glass lodged in my lower back. This one was deeper, and I jerked a tiny bit.

"He kept calling me sister and little wolf. I think he thought I was like you. A lycanthrope."

Billy Bob stopped then. He took my shoulders with both his hands and gently turned me. "What else did he say?"

"Weird stuff, like he wasn't my enemy and that I shouldn't be afraid of him." But I hadn't needed several weeks of torture to know bullshit when I heard it. "I can't remember it all." I caught Billy Bob's eyes flicker toward my naked breasts. He'd seen them before. He'd seen all of me before on his surgical table and during the many exams I'd had to endure. But I'd never seen him look at me, or them, like this—with heat.

I crossed my arms over my chest and waited for his gaze to meet mine.

"I'm sorry," he said. "We should get you back to the house."

"I don't..."

"You will sleep in my room, and I will not leave you tonight."

I tucked my chin, "In your room?"

"I will stay in the chair. I won't be sleeping. Your safety is my only concern."

"If it's the killer, he knows where I am now."

"If it's the killer, he'll have more than he bargained for if he tries to get to you again." He wiped my cheek with his thumb. "Let's shift, or it's going to be a long trip back. You covered several miles."

"Really?"

He chuckled. "Really." In the next few moments, I watched Billy Bob transform with a fluid elegance I'd never seen in another therian. It dawned on me, as I gaped at his large wolf covered in thick silvery fur that I'd never seen him shift before. Frankly, I found him unsettlingly striking. He waited, his gray eyes expectant. I nodded, concentrated on my coyote, and changed again. I'd never shifted twice in the same night. Hell, most of the time I only changed on the full moon. It was surprisingly easier than before. I could have probably followed my scent trail back to the house, but I let Billy Bob take the lead.

CHAPTER 4

I WOKE ON CUE AT FIVE in the morning. My internal clock had adjusted to my work schedule. There was no such thing as a short day for a small business owner. I looked at the chair where Billy Bob slept. Irrationally, I was relieved and irritated. I'd told him I didn't need a watch-dog, or in this case a watch-wolf. I didn't want to admit, even to myself, that the only reason I could sleep was because he was in the room with me. I hated my treacherous emotions for making me feel safe when he was near.

He'd worn blue-striped pajama bottoms to sleep in and no shirt. His arms were crossed as if he was still on watch, but his eyes were closed. I studied the hard planes of his face, his wide cheekbones, his almond-shaped eyes, and his full, wide lips. Christ on a hot plate, why did he have to be so fucking handsome? His grandfather had been a shaman for their pack. He'd told me that once when I'd first moved to Peculiar. Now he was the shaman for a town full of therianthropes.

At the time, I'd been searching for Judah, and Billy Bob had been one of the few people who believed his disappearance might be foul play. I'd even told him about Sunny. About her psychic gifts. He hadn't thought I was crazy. Though, like my brother, Babel, he'd tried to talk me out of bringing her here. I knew he didn't feel that way now. They'd both fallen hard for Sunny, and why wouldn't they, she was easy to love.

The throw blanket slid down Billy Bob's chest, and I sighed. Happily. *Damn it, hormones!* Rodin might as well have sculpted his broad shoulders and wide chest. I knew he was at least fifty, maybe even older, but he looked like someone in the prime of their late twenties, early thirties. His silvery gray hair always made him seem older. I wondered if it had been that color his whole life or if it had turned that way over the years.

I swallowed the lump in my throat. *I will not stare. I will not stare.* I couldn't stop myself, though. No amount of mantra was going to drag my gaze from his super yummy body. I needed to focus elsewhere, but the other stuff on my mind was just too grisly and awful.

I focused my thoughts on other tasks than the hunky werewolf in the room. Billy Bob had told me that he still needed the dental records from a dentist in Lake Ozarks to compare against the victim's, but he'd been mostly certain that the man killed was my friend Ruth Thompson's gentle and sweet husband Ed. When I had gone up to my apartment to change and shower, they'd removed the body. Underneath the corpse, the killer had left Ed's driver's license. The height and weight had been right. Billy Bob had typed the victim's blood, and that had matched as well.

I squeezed my eyes shut trying to block out the vision of murder. When I opened them, Billy Bob was staring at me. Turnabout, and all that.

"What is it?"

"What?"

"You're crying."

"No, I'm not." I scrubbed at the wetness on my cheeks.

"Okay." He rose from the chair. "You're safe, Chavvah. I promise I won't let anyone or anything hurt you." I could hear the implied, *not again*.

I tried not to read too much into his declaration. He was a good man. Sunny had told me that more than once, along with Ruth. Just about everyone in town loved the doctor. It grated on my nerves. No one was that perfect. How a lycan had managed to ingratiate himself into a town full of therianthropes was completely beyond me.

"How did you end up in Peculiar?" I asked Billy Bob.

"Long story."

"I have a few minutes."

He smiled, but it didn't reach his eyes. His gorgeous gray gaze held a pain that made me ache to comfort him. Stop it, I told myself. The doc had women throwing themselves at him all the time, council member Bethany included. Damn it. I'd almost managed to forget about the snide little fox.

"Chav…"

"If you don't want to tell me, you don't have to." I grabbed my phone from the nightstand and rolled over to face the opposite wall. I couldn't look at him. I don't know why his reluctance to share his past hurt, but it did. "I need a few minutes. I need to call Jo Jo and Sunny to let them know what happened. I don't want them showing up this morning and stumbling on that awful bloody pool out back."

"Especially not Sunny," Billy Bob said.

The skin on my face tightened. "Yeah, especially Sunny." Sunny's gift had been out of whack since Jude's birth so she might not get any visions, but there was no sense in taking a chance. Besides, she'd never been good with blood. It usually made her pass out.

"I'll get coffee on." Billy Bob didn't bother to put on a shirt. He just walked to the closed door. "Do you want any breakfast?"

My brain chose that moment to flash an image of the skinned corpse splayed in the dirt. Nausea roiled. "No, thanks." How on earth could I cook today with that memory replaying in my mind?

He nodded. "Come to the kitchen when you're ready."

"You got it, doc."

After he had left, I called Sunny.

"Hello," she said after two rings.

"Hi, sorry. I hope I didn't wake you."

"No worries, Chav. Baby Jude beat you to the punch."

I could hear her glider squeaking now. "I...I don't know how to tell you this."

"Just say it, Chav. You know I don't like tip-toeing around bad news."

"Someone...died." Damn it! The details stuck in my throat.

"Who?" she asked.

"Doc isn't sure yet, but—"

"What do you mean, he isn't sure yet? Is it one of the people in for the Jubilee?" My heart squeezed at the small hope in her voice.

I automatically shook my head even though she couldn't see me. "He thinks it's a local."

"Who?"

"It's so bad, Sunny."

"Not Jo Jo." Her words were tense with fear.

"No, not him."

"Take a deep breath, Chav, and tell me."

How could I say Ed's name? We didn't know for sure that it was him. It could be someone else. A stranger. I felt heartsick knowing how relieved I'd feel if it was a stranger. "Billy Bob can't be sure yet, and I don't want to say something that might not be true."

There was a muffled, "Wake up, Babe. Something's happened in town." Then a clearer, "Where are you now?"

"I'm at the doc's place."

There was a moment of silence. "All night?"

"The sheriff didn't want me to stay in the apartment after—" My mouth watered as I tried to control the emotion in my voice. "Someone skinned him, Sunny. They skinned him like an animal and slit his throat at the back of our restaurant. I was in the kitchen when…" My voice went up an octave as my horror renewed. "I was right there, by the door, where the body was dumped."

"I'm coming," Sunny said. "Babe and I will pick you up in thirty minutes."

* * * *

I took my time getting dressed. I didn't want to face Billy Bob.

Be strong, little wolf.

The voice startled me. I turned my head sharply left then right. I was alone in the room, but I'd heard it. I'd heard *him*, the intruder from the night before. Only, I hadn't because I was alone. *It's just the voice,* I told myself. *My stupid, stupid voice.* The master bathroom door was wide open, the shower had a see-through glass door, and the closet was closed. If the guy were hiding in the closet, he wouldn't have sounded so clear or so close.

I shook my head. My brain was playing tricks on me. It was the only explanation. Even so, I suddenly wanted to be out of the bedroom and in the kitchen with Billy Bob. Well, really, anyone. I didn't want to be alone with my thoughts or my invisible friend.

"Good morning," the doc said when I shuffled into his kitchen. He'd pulled on a sage green T-shirt that complimented his skin tone perfectly. I wondered if he'd look bad in any color.

"Morning," I said, accepting the steaming mug of coffee. "Cream and sugar?"

"Sugar's on the counter." He pointed to a white spirally sculptured sugar dish. "I'll get the cream for you." He opened the large side-by-side refrigerator and pulled a quart container from the door shelf.

The coffee had a nice, pungent, but fresh aroma and after a couple of tablespoons of raw, unrefined sugar and real heavy cream, it was as if I could smell heaven. Or at least what I hoped it smelled like.

"This is really good."

"I grind my own bean."

"Of course you do."

He let my snide comment go. "Did you get ahold of Sunny?"

"Yeah, she and Babe are on their way over to get me."

He set his cup down, a hard thump on the center island. "Are you going to go stay with them?"

I hadn't even thought about going to Sunny's since I'd suggested it the night before. Did Billy Bob want me to leave? "I don't know." I shook my head. "Probably. No worries. I'll be out of your hair soon."

"You can be such an idiot," he said.

I snapped my gaze to him and narrowed my eyes. "Excuse me."

His whole body seemed to be vibrating as he met my stare with the same angry heat. Within two heartbeats, he closed the distance between us, his arms wrapping me up as his lips melded hot over my own. My loosey-goosy arms flopped at my sides as my skin ignited with the pleasure his kiss foisted upon me. My knees buckled, but he held me up as his tongue found its way between my lips, conquering me with every thrust. He tasted of coffee, of cinnamon, the pungent scent of bergamot and spice filled my nostrils as my lower, more sensitive area throbbed with an aching need born so deep in my soul.

The doorbell rang. We ignored it, feeding the growing passion. The loud banging on the front door along with Sunny shouting my name, however, brought us both to a gasping halt.

"I…" couldn't formulate a coherent thought, let alone a complete sentence. "I…"

Billy Bob growled. "I'll get it." He let me go, and my shaking legs could barely carry me. Fuckity-fuck-

fuck. What the hell had just happened? Before I could process, Sunny stormed into the room and embraced me.

"Oh, Chavvah. I'm so sorry. This is terrible. I'm so glad you're okay. You're safe."

"Yeah." I gulped. "Safe." And horny. What the hell?

She put her hands on her ample hips, wider and curvier now that she was a mom. Seriously, she'd never looked more stunning. Her green eyes sparkled with fire as she turned to stare at Billy Bob. "Tell me what you know and don't leave anything out."

"Now, Sunny," he said. I hated how quickly he'd regained his composure. When we were alone again, he and I were going to have a serious talk. He continued, "It's an ongoing investigation. I've been brought in to do the autopsy, but I can't tell you the particulars of the case."

She snapped her fingers. "That is not going to fly with me, mister."

Babel put his arms around Sunny from behind. "Calm yourself, sweetheart."

My eyes widened, because, at that point, Sunny turned around in his arms, poked him in the chest and shook her finger at him. When Sunny did the poke and shake, she meant business. "Now, you listen here, Babel Michael Trimmel, you have to have a serious screw loose if you think telling me to calm down is the way to get me to calm down."

"I'm sorry," he said, and boy, how he was sorry. Regret for his word choice was written all over his face.

"Damn right you are." She turned back to Billy Bob. "Now give, or I'm going to storm the Sheriff's office, and since you all want me to keep low key during your furry-fest, you'd be better off telling me what I want to know."

He groaned and shook his head. Babe smartly stayed quiet.

Without meaning to, I stepped between her and Billy Bob. "Don't yell at him, Sunny." Oh my God. What was I doing? Why was I defending Billy Bob? The first rule of BFF code was you always backed your BFF.

She looked at me and raised her right brow, her lips pursed.

I looked at Billy Bob, who stared at me like I'd grown a third nipple in the middle of my forehead, and said, "Just tell her."

* * * *

After the previous night's events had been relayed, Sunny said, "So let me get this straight. A man was skinned alive, murdered, and tossed onto our back doorstep." She peered at me as she picked up my mug and sipped my coffee. "Had you locked the door?"

"Yes, I locked the door." At least I was pretty sure I had. It had been a long, exhausting day.

Babe and Billy Bob had gone just outside the kitchen to talk officially. As the mayor, Babel would need to strategize how to handle the fallout. Still, it really pissed me off. This was probably Ed. Our friend. A staple in our community. It irritated me that we had to take all these incoming strangers into any consideration when it came to dealing with his death.

"The alarm?" Sunny asked. "Did you set it?"

"I…" Had I really been so stupid? "No. I guess I forget." A wave of recrimination and remorse washed over me. Would it have made a difference if the alarms had gone off?

"Jesus, Chav. With all these strangers in town, you can't forget. It's more than just our friends and neighbors now."

"I know," I said. "Don't beat me up about it. I already feel bad enough."

"I'm sorry, doll. This was not your fault. Lock. No lock. Alarm. No alarm. When a sicko does something sick, there is no one to blame except the sicko. You didn't choose to hurt that poor man, whoever it turns out to be, and dwelling on *would'ves, could'ves,* and *what ifs* will give you gas. I just worry about you is all. I don't know what I'd do without you, you know?" Sunny hugged me again. It felt good. She really did give the best hugs.

I could feel some of the tension drain from my muscles. "I do know," I said, hugging her back. "I don't know what I'd do without you either. You always have my back."

"Always," she said fiercely. She leaned back and looked me in the face. She squinted her eyes, her brow furrowing. "Why is your face so red?"

I hadn't realized it was, but her mentioning it brought a fresh rise of heat to my cheeks. Sunny's eyes widened as she took in my guilty expression. She glanced once at Billy Bob out in the hall talking quietly with Babel now. To her grace, she didn't say anything. However, I knew an interrogation would be forthcoming.

Babe and Billy Bob walked back into the room, neither of them looking as if they'd figured out anything.

"We need to tell Sunny," Babe said.

"Tell me what?" Sunny asked.

"Who the victim might be."

"Ed," Billy Bob said, his tone low and fierce. "It might be Ed Thompson."

The blood drained from Sunny's face. She slumped onto one of the high stools next to the center island. "No," she said. "It can't be." She stared at me, her eyes pleading with me to refute Billy Bob.

I shook my head.

Her reaction was similar to mine. "We just saw him yesterday. He came in for lunch. How can it be Ed?" She gripped my wrist. "How could I have missed it? What good is it for me to have a psychic gift when I can't even use it to save my friends?"

"This isn't your fault, sweetheart," Babe said. He massaged her shoulders, and she slumped back against him, drawing comfort from her husband.

"Babe's right, Sunny. This isn't your fault."

An infant's cry from the other room brought us all to attention.

"Shoot," Sunny said, the front of her shirt darkened as her nipple fountains exploded. "I left Jude in the living room when we came in. He'd been sleeping so soundly." She looked down at her blouse. "I packed a clean one in the diaper bag."

"And nipple pads, I hope."

"Being a mother has its perks and its drawbacks," she said. Babe went with her into the other room, leaving Billy Bob and me alone.

"You holding up?" he asked, careful to keep to his side of the island.

I nodded. Why had he kissed me earlier? Had he felt sorry for me? Remembering his hands kneading my back, his lips seeking mine, his tongue exploring my tonsils, I knew the passion hadn't been one sided. "Should we talk about what happened?"

"Not now," he said.

Well, *motherfuck*! Seriously? "Cool," I said. "Actually, we don't ever have to talk about it. Let's pretend like it never happened. As a matter of fact..." I shook my head. "...I just scrubbed it from my brain. We're good."

"Chavvah." He made my name sound like a warning.

Sunny and Babe came back into the kitchen and saved me from more humiliation.

"Can you guys take me home?" I glanced at the now glowering Billy Bob. "We need to get the restaurant figured out, or we need to ask Blondina to cover the food for the council meeting. Either way, there is a lot to do." I didn't add that I desperately wanted to get out of sight of a certain asshole werewolf who kept sending me mixed signals.

Billy Bob interceded. "I think you should stay here, Chavvah."

"Not happening, Doc." I sounded terse and emotional. Why wouldn't he just let me have what was left of my tattered dignity?

"At least, let me examine your back before you go. A few of those cuts were pretty deep."

"You were hurt?" Babe said with a pinch of alarm. "Doctor Smith didn't say that you were attacked." It was my younger brother's turn to glower.

"I threw myself out of the guest bedroom window last night." And I didn't want to fucking talk about it. "It's a long story. I'll explain later. Right now, I want to go." For emphasis, I added, "Please."

Sunny took me by the arm, her hand just above the scar on my elbow. "Give me some of that famous salve of yours, Billy Bob. I'll get Chavvah taken care of when we get back to the cabin."

"No," he said. "I'll examine her before she goes."

"You're not the boss of me," I told him as if we were five-year-olds.

"I am your doctor. The laceration in your lower back needs a second look. I want to make sure it's healing well before you go."

He knew I was a shifter and that I would heal better than any human with a cut. I looked at his face and gauged his stubborn expression. Damn it. He wasn't going to take "no" for an answer, but I'd be damned if I gave him a "yes." I didn't want to be alone with him right now.

"Chavvie, just let him take a look."

"Fine," I huffed. I yanked my shirt over my head and turned my back to Billy Bob. I was wearing a bra, but Babe still turned around to face the living room. Sunny walked around the backside of me to see how bad I'd been injured.

"It looks decent," she said brightly. "Already scabbing up."

I didn't wait for the doc's verdict. I grabbed my shirt off the center island. "Let's get on out of here."

"Thank you, Billy Bob," I heard Sunny say when I was halfway to the front door. "I appreciate you taking such good care of Chav last night." I glanced back in time to see her go up on her tip-toes and kiss his cheek. She said something too quietly for me to hear, but he gave her a quick nod then went back into the kitchen and out of sight.

CHAPTER 5

"I REALLY DON'T KNOW what more I can tell you, Sheriff." I let out a frustrated sigh. It was a bit after nine in the morning, and I'd felt as if I'd been there for decades. "Other than his fight with Mike Wares, nothing suspicious happened." Sheriff Taylor had called me shortly after Sunny, Babe, and I got back to their cabin around six a.m. After he'd insisted that I come down to give a statement, I showered while Sunny took care of calling Jo Jo to tell him to take the day off. Even still, I'd made good time getting to the sheriff's station.

Sheriff Taylor pinched the bridge of his nose. "Chavvah, it hurts nothing to go over what happened last night. Or yesterday in the restaurant for that matter. So Mike said he'd see Ed rot? Did you feel like it was a genuine threat?" I'd told him all about Mike and his threats in the restaurant now that I knew the victim might be Ed, and we'd rehashed it a gazillion million times.

"I don't know. Mike's a hot head. We all know that. I'd be surprised if Ed were the only person he fought with yesterday." Even so, I found it hard to believe the bear shifter had skinned someone alive and sliced his throat. That wasn't a skill you learned by accident. "Have you ever heard of Mike being cruel to animals?

Sheriff Taylor shook his head, but out loud, he said, "Did anyone else suspicious come in? Did you notice anything else wrong before you tripped over…" He paused. I could see the weariness and grief in his downturned mouth and heavy-lidded eyes. "It's okay," he finally said. "I just hoped…"

I patted his hand when he put it on his desk. "I'll keep trying to remember something. I promise." I steeled my courage to say the next part. "I'm assuming you sent someone over to Ruth and Ed's last night."

He nodded his head.

"And?"

"And Ed was called to tow a broken-down truck in from Lake Ozark last night. He got the call around five-thirty, left near six, and Ruth hasn't had contact with him since. He left his cell phone in the garage. Ruth says he does that sometimes."

"Did you tell her about…?"

"Yes," Sheriff Taylor said. "She's a hard lady to keep secrets from."

He wasn't kidding. Ruth could get me to spill just about anything. Twenty years as a parent to seven kids had taught her a trick or two. "You should tell Tyler. It isn't right for him to accidentally overhear his father might be, you know, through cop gossip."

"Ruth has asked that I keep it under wraps until we're certain the body is Ed's. I'm going to take her to Dr. Smith's this afternoon. She insisted on going for a viewing, even though I'm not sure there's anything left of him that's identifiable other than his teeth."

"I'll go with you. She'll need support during this, and I've already seen more than anyone else should. Still, however, this works out, Deputy Thompson is not going to thank you for keeping him in the dark."

"I know." He shook his head, the dark circles around his eyes more prominent than I'd ever seen. "But it's my call. Right now, the only people who know it might be Ed is Doc Smith, Mark Smart, you…though the doc shouldn't have told you…and me. I didn't even tell Farraday, so there will be no talking about it."

I kept it to myself that Babe and Sunny also knew. "Things like this don't stay secret for long, Sheriff." I stood up. "I'm going to Ruth's house. I'll see you in a little bit."

He hadn't told me I could go, but he hadn't told me I couldn't either. In a way, I think he was grateful to share the burden of Ruth with someone else. I opened the door to his office and quickly found Tyler in the bullpen talking to the handsome man from the diner, Dominic Tartan. The one I'd made a lunch date with. I tensed when the man noticed me and smiled. The joy zinged right to his eyes, and I'll admit that I was charmed. Behind him were the other two men who'd ordered lunch with him. Hans Something-Or-Another and Randy Lowry. Randy smiled as well. However, Hans didn't seem to notice me.

"Chavvah," he said as he and Tyler approached. "How are you?" He asked it in a congenial, *I have no idea you tripped over a dead body and had to spend the night locked down with a man that constantly raised your ire*, way.

"Fine." I nodded. "Dominic, right?"

"Call me Dom. I'm pleased you remembered." His green gaze met mine. "We're still on for Sunday, right?"

I wanted to tell him "no," but I would've had to explain why, and I wanted to explain even less than I wanted to back out of our lunch date. "Sure." I gave him a tight-lipped smile because it was all I could muster under the circumstances.

A woman sashayed into the Sheriff's office. She had curves for days and fiery red hair to go with her fiery expression. She raised an eyebrow at Dom and his cohorts.

"Well?" she asked.

"Wilhelmina," the Hans guy said, his voice slightly accented. "I told you we'd take care of this."

"Look," she said, snapping her fingers at him. "Jerry might not have been a peach, but he wouldn't take off without a word."

"Who?" I asked.

Randy Lowry moved closer to me. "You definitely don't want to get in the middle of this," he said conspiratorially. He pointed to the redhead. "That's Willy Boden. Hans's sister. She's security for the therian council, and that hair isn't just window dressing. She has a hot temper. Jerry Blackwell is her sometimes boyfriend and fellow delegate from the Kansas group. They represent the *Felidae* of their state."

"Feel-a-day?"

"*Felidae*," he said again. "Big cats. In their case, pumas."

"Ah." In other words, mountain lion shifters like Rose Ann Corman, Jo Jo's mother, had been. "She seems pretty peeved."

"Apparently, Jerry took off the day we arrived and hasn't been back."

A shiver rippled through me. "Three days ago?" Why were they just reporting it now?

"He and Willy got into a huge fight," he explained without me asking.

"Hmm." I pursed my lips then looked at him. His brown eyes were full of mirth. "Why are you telling me all this?"

He smiled, his brown eyes glittering with intensity. "I like having a reason to talk to you."

"Oh." I blushed.

"I only wished I'd been quicker than Dom in asking you out." He nudged me familiarly. "Watch out for that one. From what I hear, he never stays in one place too long or with any one girl."

"You really are straight forward." And slick, like Dom, in his own way. I bit my lip nervously. I hadn't been flirted with by any man in a long time, and now I had two flirting hardcore.

"Life's too short. I believe in pursuing something when I really want it."

I think I must have looked like a deer in the headlights because he suddenly laughed. "Have a nice day, Ms. Trimmel. It was a pleasure to see you again."

"Uh huh." I gave him a crisp wave. "I've got to go. See you around."

He flashed a brilliant smile. "Count on it."

I nodded to Farraday and Connelly, who sat at their desks typing up reports or something to that effect, as I passed by. Before I got to the exit, a hand on my shoulder stopped me. I turned to see Tyler Thompson.

"You okay, Chav?" He and my brother Judah had been best friends at one time until they had a falling out. Which meant, eventually, I would forgive him for being uncharitable to Sunny when she'd arrived in town. He'd been a dick because he was afraid she'd expose a secret affair between his mother and Judah with her psychic visions. An affair that *never* happened, I might add. It had made me so angry when I'd found out, but as I stared at him now, all I could feel was pity.

"I am," I told him. "Have you been by to see your mom today?"

"No." He gave me a puzzled look. "Why?"

"No reason. I'll talk to you later." And without waiting for his response, I made a hasty exit.

* * * *

It was almost ten a.m. when I wandered up to Ruth's yard. The Thompson's two-story home was just on the other side of their garage. The yard was neatly trimmed and green from all the frequent rain storms we'd had in June. The border up the driveway was lush with purple irises and orange tiger lilies. Bright fuschia peonies added more splashes of color. Near the mailbox was a large wisteria bush, and the day's heat had the sweet odor clinging to the air. The splendor only added to my trepidation. I didn't want to do this, be the one who comforted Ruth in her time of need. I wasn't sure I was strong enough to hold up for her.

Buck up, I told myself. I didn't have to be strong. I just had to pretend to be long enough to help my friend. Ruth had been there for me after my rescue, and I'd been damned if I would allow myself to act like a coward.

The screen door banged open, and a small tawny-haired boy ran out the door. He nearly ran me down as he passed. "Linus!" I said.

He turned his head back to look at me, a cheeky smile on his face. "Gotta go, Aunt Chav. He shook a handful of coins in his pants pocket. "Mom said I could go down to Riverfront Street. They got some carnival booths set up with games." He was small for his age, only eight-years-old now, and I wished I could freeze-frame the look of joy on his sweet face.

I smiled at him. "Go on then."

He rose up on his tip-toes in a quick moment of triumph and took off down the street in a sprint. My stomach hurt. I almost turned around and headed out as well. Why was this happening to such good people?

I shook my head as I thought the question. Bad people did bad things to good people all the time. Being good didn't make a person immune to evil. Shivering, I rubbed my upper arms. This murder had been evil like I'd never seen, and I'd seen more than my fair share.

I stared at the screen door. Linus hadn't closed the main one. There was a light on, and I heard a soft whimper. *Ruth*. My heart broke even more. I lifted my shoulders and straightened my back, and by making myself place one foot in front of the other, I headed toward the house.

When I got the screen, I opened the door and said, "Ruth." I stepped inside and let the door close behind me. "Ruth. It's Chavvah."

She appeared in the hall by the living room, her eyes and nose both red, her usually flawless skin, blotchy. She sniffled. "What are you doing here?"

"I wanted to be here for you."

She looked at me, mild surprise in her grieved expression. "Who told you?"

Oh, God. She didn't know I'd been the one to find the body. How much had Sheriff Taylor told Ruth? "Are all the kids out? I just passed Linus."

She nodded. "Dakota and Michele are with my parents in Branson for the day. The rest are down on Riverfront Street for the Jubilee. I already texted Emma Ray and told her to keep an eye out for Linus." She sat on the arm of the divan, her delicate features making her appear fragile, but I knew she wasn't.

Ruth Thompson was one of the strongest women I knew.

"I found the…" I shook my head and tried again. "It happened at the restaurant after closing last night. I found … I went outside to take the trash and … I wish the sheriff would have told you."

She gulped, her head bobbing as if nodding agreement. "Do you think it's him?"

I shrugged, the gesture wholly inadequate for the situation. A sweet smell wafted in from the kitchen. It had a strange but familiar bite to it. "What is that?"

"What?"

"The smell?" I followed the scent into the kitchen. Ruth made her family breakfast every morning. I know, because I often joined them. The room always smelled of home cooking. Not today. Instead, it was the spicy, sweet, and pungent scent I'd smelled the night before. I let my coyote slip forward and inhaled deeply. Strangely, my senses seemed sharper, more acute and I nearly gagged as the scent-memory took me back to the scene of the murder.

"Chavvah, tell me what you're trailing?" As a deer shifter, Ruth's olfactory senses weren't as developed as mine, but how could she not smell this?

I spotted a clear jar filled with what looked like wood chips about the color of raw almonds. "What is that?"

"Sassafras root," she said. "Why?"

"I smelled it, Ruth." My skin tightened with a shiver. "At the restaurant last night. I smelled this." Even over the scent of exposed flesh and blood. Although, I didn't say so. Was it significant? Did this prove the dead man was Ed? Had he chewed it before he'd been killed? Had the aroma come from his mouth?

"Butch won it this morning from one of the carnival games. The street fair opened up around eight today. He brought it home and then grabbed his brother and sisters to go back. Except for Linus."

"Then Ed wouldn't have eaten it last night?"

"Ed doesn't even like root beer, let alone sassafras. He says it's too much like licorice." She put her hand to her mouth. "Ed didn't like it." Her creamy complexion turned a milky white as the blood drained from her face.

"Sit down," I told her. I pulled out a chair from the table. "We don't know it's him."

"In all the years we've been married, he has never not come home and never not called if he was going to be late. This isn't like him, Chav." A choking sob rose in her throat. "I can't lose him. I just can't."

A kick at the door had us both turning to the noise. A man stood on the other side of the kitchen screen door, scraping debris off his boots onto a mud mat. He lifted his head and pushed his way inside. "Can't lose who, Ruthie? Did something happen to one of the kids?"

My throat grew thick. Ruth jumped up, knocking her chair off its legs. "Ed!" she shouted. Relief, disbelief, joy—and just a touch of anger—colored her voice. She launched herself into his arms and kissed him hard, intimate. I tried to fight the grin on my face but gave up after Ed's arms wrapped around her, and they both decided they were the only two people in the room.

Before they could drop their clothes, I cleared my throat.

Ed set Ruth down, the biggest, dreamiest smile on his face. "If I'd have known getting stuck in Timbuktu would create this kind of reaction, I would have done it much sooner."

Ruth's face turned red. Ed had said exactly the wrong thing. "You jerk!" she yelled. "I thought you were dead. Dead!" She beat her fist on his chest. "They told me—" She wheezed in a breath. "They told me!" she accused him.

Ed pulled his wife into an encapsulating embrace, keeping a good hold as she fought against him. He kept saying things over and over, like, "I'm all right. It's all right. There, there. I'm here."

When Ruth stopped struggling, he just held her while she sobbed into his chest.

"Chavvah, what's happening?" he asked me as he stroked his wife's hair. "Why did you all think I was dead?"

"I found a body last night. He was out back of the restaurant. The sheriff thought it might be you."

"Did he look like me?"

"No." I shook my head as if trying to shake the memory. "He didn't look like anyone."

Ed's expression grew puzzled. "Then why me?"

Ruth leaned back. "Because the man had been skinned alive, your ID was under the body, and you didn't fucking come home last night!"

Whoa. Ed's shocked expression must have reflected my own. I think that was the first time I'd ever heard Ruth cuss. Ed and I were both smart enough to keep our comments on her uncharacteristic outburst to ourselves.

I took a shot at helpful. "I think the first thing we need to do is call the sheriff and let him know he's been barking up the wrong corpse."

Ruth put her hands on her hips. "Is that supposed to be funny?"

"Uhm." I swallowed the spit in gathering in my mouth. I phrased my response as a question. "No?" The body obviously wasn't Ed's, and the police needed to reassess their investigation.

Ruth harrumphed as she disengaged from Ed. "Where are you going?" he asked.

"To get my phone, damn it. I guess we better call the GD sheriff."

I raised a brow at Ed. "Wow," I mouthed. "She nearly went there."

He shook his head at me and sat down at the table. I noticed then how tired he looked.

"What happened to you last night?"

"I got a call to tow a vehicle from Lake Ozark to Peculiar, a council member's car. It took a while to get it hooked up right because of it being one of those fancy foreign cars. A sporty two-door with a really narrow carriage. I knew I should have called Ruth, but I had expected to be home in less than an hour once it got all situated on the back of my tow truck. But on the way home, I had two tires blow out. Don't know how that happened. Anyhow, I was between here and Lake Ozarks, and it was going to be a twenty-mile walk no matter which way I played it."

"And you left your phone in the garage."

"Yeah." He nodded. "That too."

"You could have shifted. It would have been a much quicker trip."

"I supposed I could have." He pulled his wallet from his back pocket and set it on the table. "But I didn't want to leave this behind, and really, I thought someone would come along and give me a ride into town."

"Well, you scared the shit out of all of us. Where did the killer get your driver's license from anyways?"

He furrowed his brow and opened his wallet. "It's not in here."

"When did you last use it?"

"It must have fallen out when I paid for lunch yesterday."

"Can it really just be a coincidence that your ID was under the dead guy?"

"Those are questions for the Sheriff's department, Chavvah," Sheriff Taylor said when he walked into the kitchen with Ruth. "This is an official investigation, and beyond a witness statement, you need to stay out of it."

I didn't fight the heavy sigh that went with my disappointment. I stood up. "Fine. I'm glad you're okay, Ed." I turned to Ruth and gave her a quick hug. In her ear, I whispered, "Call me later to compare notes."

She whispered back, "You got it."

I nodded to the sheriff who looked less burdened. He had known Ed his whole life and having to think his friend was dead, murdered so awfully, had taken its toll. "I'll let you know if I think of anything else."

He gave me a two-finger salute. "Do that," he said.

I shouldn't have, but as I walked out of the Thompson house, I felt lighter, even more than before the murder. It was as if the scorecard of my life finally had a checked "win" box for once. My friend was alive. He was with his family and not a bloody skinned, eyeball-less corpse on Billy Bob's slab. Someone was dead. That hadn't changed, and even through my relief, I was determined to find out who had been left for me to find.

CHAPTER 6

MAIN STREET WAS PACKED with therians from all over Missouri, Arkansas, and Kansas. I think a few might have even come in from Oklahoma, even though they weren't a part of the Tri-State Council. The news of the murder must not have gotten out yet because no one seemed frightened or alarmed as they jovially shopped the local stores and the many craft booths set up around town.

Elton Brown smiled when I walked past his furniture shop. He was helping a non-local load up a unique hand carved side table. Some of his furniture was antique, but some he made himself. The craftsmanship on this one was special.

"That's gorgeous, Elton," I said as he helped the young woman close the tailgate on her small truck.

"Thanks, Chav." His whole demeanor was more cheerful than I'd ever seen him. "I can't believe how many custom made pieces I'm selling." He lowered his voice. "And these people don't mind paying for quality."

"As they should," I said. His happiness infected me, that and Ed being alive, gave me a sense of hope. I saw a basket full of ornate walking sticks. "Are those yours too?"

"Yes," he said. "I've sold a half dozen in the past three days. I think this week is going to go a long way to paying for the new addition off the back of the store. It'll be nice to have my workshop so close."

"I'm glad for you, Elton. Real glad."

"Thanks, Chavvah." He put his hands on his hips in a very Superman kind of way. "I think things are finally turning around for me."

"I'm glad." I waved good-bye and headed for Sunny's Outlook. I really didn't want to go into the restaurant, but my need to get into my apartment for my car keys outweighed my need to avoid.

Just past the courthouse, someone shouted my name. "Chavvah!"

When I looked up, Dominic Tartan was striding toward me. He smiled, waving as he wound his way through the morning Jubilee crowd.

"Hey," I said when he stood in front of me. I smiled, slowly raising my gaze to meet his.

Hubba, as Sunny would say. This was one handsome man. His features reminded me of a muscular, more handsome, less pretty Johnny Depp. In the bright sunlight, his eyes were the color of the inside flesh of an exquisitely ripe California avocado. They were light, opaque yellowish-green around the pupils and a darker green on the outside edge of the irises. I'd never seen anyone with that eye color. "Is it already Sunday?"

"I wish." He hesitated and then gestured to the festivities. "Do you want to walk down to Riverfront with me and check out the Jubilee?"

"I…I don't know." Going with him was probably a bad idea, but I was flattered by the attention. I wasn't sure I was ready to go back to the restaurant and my apartment yet, anyhow. Besides, Dom wasn't playing games with me, like a certain werewolf I won't name.

"I promise to win you a stuffed animal," he said.

I laughed. "I don't know how I can say no to such a generous offer." I cocked a brow. "Throw in a corn dog and a fresh squeezed lemonade, and you got yourself a deal."

"You drive a hard bargain, Chavvah Trimmel." He grinned. "I like that in a woman."

I flushed with pleasure and took his arm when he offered it. Twelfth Street to Riverfront was less busy than Main. It was a short two-block walk, but my left leg started to ache from all the activity. I hated feeling like a weakling.

"Something wrong?" Dominic asked.

"No," I said. I didn't want to admit to him that I hurt because that would entail telling him about my past. For Dominic, I didn't want to be the girl who'd been kidnapped and tortured for three weeks. Right then, I didn't want to be the girl who tripped over a body the evening before. I wanted to be the girl a guy like Dom wanted to woo. "I just got a hitch in my giddy-up. Must have slept wrong last night." Not a complete lie.

"Well, it hasn't taken away from your beauty." He turned his gaze to me. "You are lovely, Chavvah. Uniquely beautiful. Your name as well." He furrowed his brow. "Does it mean something? It sounds almost Native American."

"It's actually biblical," I said with an easy smile. It wasn't the first time someone mistook my name for something more exotic than what it was. It's Hebrew for 'breath of life'."

"Are you Jewish?"

I snorted. "No, but my parents a die-hard Christians. They named my brothers and me after names they found in a Hebrew baby names book. They wanted to take it Old Testament with us."

"It's really lovely."

"Thanks." I shrugged.

Riverfront Street, the first and oldest street in Peculiar, still had the original paving laid down from more than eighty years ago. The rectangular brick-like stones gave the area an authentic old-timey charm. It made me glad the town kept this part of its history.

I saw Selena Messer holding hands with Deputy Connelly. Who would have thought two very different types of therians could be soul mates? My friend Sunny Haddock, that's who. She'd told me about the vision she'd had of those two, and it made me warm with a strange kind of joy.

"See something you like?" Dominic asked.

"Yes," I said. I pointed to Selena and Connelly. "Those two. They shouldn't work, but they do."

"Why's that?"

"Bear," I said, indicating Selena then gestured to the Deputy. "Squirrel."

Dominic laughed, his mirth rich with timbre. "This town is full of surprises."

The sudden scent of sassafras darkened my mood. "No kidding." Damn it. I'd forgotten to tell the sheriff about the smell. As we walked past game booth after game booth, the perfume of sassafras mingled with corn dogs, sausages, hamburgers, funnel cakes, and a variety of drinks.

I was so intent on finding the booth that gave away the flavored root bark, I tripped over Linus and knocked a genuine root beer from the kid's hand.

"Aunt Chav!" he said.

"Crap." My purse was still back at the apartment. "I'm sorry. I don't have any money on me to get you another one."

Dominic pulled a five-dollar bill out of his wallet and handed it to the kid. "Don't spend it all in one place."

Linus snatched it quickly, and with a perfunctory "Thanks!" he ran toward another game booth.

"You didn't have to do that," I told him.

He smiled, the right side of mouth tugging slightly higher than the left in a flirty way that really worked for him. "Does it make you think more kindly of me?"

I chuckled. "Why, yes. I think it does."

"Then it was five dollars well-spent."

"Where are you from? Arkansas, right?"

"Yes," he said. "Near the Green Mountains."

"And what kind of therian are you?"

He brushed his fingers through his light brown curls. "Black Bear," he said. "You're coyote, right?"

"Yes," I said, surprised he could tell. I remembered the comment I made about Selena and Connelly. I wondered what my parents would think if I dated a bear shifter. They'd certainly like it better than me dating a wolf. "I'd have never guessed you were a bear."

"It's true what they say." He wiggled his brows. "We're good cuddlers."

I laughed hard then. Dom really put me at ease. "Did you find that Jerry guy?" Now that I knew Ed was alive, the identity of the corpse was still a question to be answered. What if it was poor Jerry that had ended up by my Dumpster?

"No, not yet," he said.

"Does he disappear a lot?"

Dom shrugged. "If he pissed off Willy then he's smart for taking off. That woman is hell on wheels."

"Oh, I can tell there's a story there." I chuckled. "She's an ex."

"Something like that, but I really don't want to talk about Willy. I'd rather focus on you." He gave me his arm again, and I gladly accepted. "The lake is nice. It must be great living in this community. The area is perfect for privacy."

Okay, then. It appeared the conversation about Willy Boden was over.

"Yeah," I said. "It's nice." When people weren't getting murdered. On the surface, Peculiar seemed like a quiet town, but I knew all too well what kind of awful could hide in a place like this.

"Oh!" he said. "There's a BB Gun shooting game. I used to be really good at clearing out the star target. How about we start there on my quest for your prize?"

I patted his arm with my free hand, and he covered it with his. "Sounds like we have a plan."

The noise was almost deafening the closer we got the game. Kyle Avery had one of the air rifles aimed at a target, and the teenager was diligently grouping his shots in small bursts to take out the star. I purposely bumped up against him when Dominic and I strolled up to the counter. His BBs went awry, and he turned on me with a growl. I glared at him until he looked away like a whipped pup. I hadn't forgotten what he'd put Sunny through the week of her wedding. She might have forgiven him, but I hadn't.

Kyle put his rifle down, picked up a jar of brown wood chips that I hadn't seen, and began to walk away.

"Hey," I said.

He turned, his eyes respectfully cast to the ground. Smart boy. He'd recently graduated from high school, and he and his mom were trying to make a go of Paw-On Pawn Shop. The ex-owner, Jeremiah Bowers, another guy killed in Peculiar, deservedly so, had been using Kyle and some of his friends to rob nearby towns. When Bowers was stupid enough to steal my grandmother's wedding rings, my Great Aunt Erma took matters into her own hands.

"Where'd you get that jar of sassafras?" I asked Kyle.

"I didn't steal it," he said defensively.

"Well, duh. Answer the question." Exasperation colored my tone.

"They're selling sassafras at the cotton candy and kettle corn stand at the end of the street. My mom wanted some."

"Thanks." I turned back to the BB Gun stand, effectively dismissing the kid.

"What was that all about?" Dominic asked.

"Oh, just an old grudge." I smiled. "Nothing I can't handle."

"I do love an assertive woman."

Damn, this guy was smooth. "You certainly know how to charm, Mr. Tartan."

"It's easy to be charming in such excellent company, Ms. Trimmel." He picked up the air rifle the vendor handed him. "Now, which stuffed animal would you like?"

I pointed to the biggest most ridiculous looking giraffe—the grand prize—and grinned. "That one."

He grinned back. "Challenge accepted."

Dominic Tartan turned out to be a man of his word, and lucky me, I got to lug a giant giraffe around by the neck. About the time we got to the corn dog stand, his phone whistled. He pulled it from his front pocket.

"Shoot." He frowned. "I've got to get over to the courthouse. The Tri-Council president has called an emergency session."

"Well, duty calls," I said. "Do you know what it's about?"

"Apparently, they have officially proclaimed Jerry missing."

"Oh." I wondered again about the skinned body. Foreboding settled heavy in my stomach. What if Jerry was the one on the doc's autopsy table?

A scream raised the hair on the back of my neck. My knee jerk reaction was to run away from whatever terror had brought on the high-pitched wail. Instead, I let my fear act as a bolster to my courage and ran toward the commotion. A crowd gathered down by the lakeshore. Blondina Messer, the owner of Blonde Bear Café, held her daughter Selena as Deputy Connelly went into crowd-control mode. His eyes met mine in a kind of plea. I nodded to him, pulled out my phone, and hit call on the screen.

"Sheriff," I said. "You better get down to Riverfront." I could see a body, red and bloated, floating near the shore. "Call Mark and Doc Smith, too."

Numb from my fingers to my toes, I swayed where I stood. Two strong arms wrapped around me and held me up.

Dominic said, "What is that?" The awe in his voice matched my shock.

"It's a person," I told him. I hugged the stuffed giraffe to my chest. "It's…"

"Whoa." His grip on me tightened, and I wasn't sure if it was for my comfort or for his own, but I didn't resist his hold. "Who? How? Why…"

"That remains to be seen."

"What's going on?"

- 96 -

I turned to see Randy Lowry standing behind us.

"It looks like a body in the river," Dom said.

"Wow," Lowry said. "He just floated up."

"Or she," I countered. It was hard to tell from this distance.

"Chance," someone shouted.

I looked and saw, again, Randy Lowry. "What the hell," I muttered.

Randy put his hand on the shoulder of a man identical to him. "Hey, Chavvah. I see you met my brother Chance."

"Identical twins?" I noticed now that Chance was thinner than his brother, but they both had boyishly handsome faces.

"Since birth," he joked. He put his arm around his brother's shoulders. "Chance is twelve minutes younger than me." His ring, a silver cube overlaid with a rotated gold cube, flashed brightly under the midday sun. Chance had one as well, only his was gold with a silver inlay. Or was it platinum. It was definitely bright enough to catch the sun's rays.

"Fancy," I said and blocked the glare with my hand.

"Twin rings from our father for our coming of age when we turned eighteen." He smiled, his eyes dancing with humor. He squeezed his brother's shoulder. "Speaking of Dad. He sent me to get you. The Tri-Council is meeting, and he wants us there for support."

Chance's eyes darkened. "I really want to see what's going on by the lake."

"We can't," Randy said. "We agreed to help the old man." He smiled at his brother. "Come on. You never know. It could prove to be an interesting meeting."

The exchange between the two brothers wasn't strange exactly, but I didn't understand Chance's reluctance to go. Maybe he and his father were in a bad place. I could sympathize with parental disappointment.

"I'll catch up with you both," Dominic said. He held up his phone and flashed the text he'd received. "It looks like we're all on the clock now."

I had stopped paying attention to Dom and the Lowry Brothers and started watching the crime scene chaos. Through the small sea of Jubilee attendees, one stood out among the crowd ... by several inches. Billy Bob was talking to Connelly now, and I couldn't help but wonder how he'd gotten to Riverfront so quickly. Then I saw *her*. Bethany Hilliard. The stupid fox shifter he'd entertained the day before was draped on his side as if he were wearing her. My muscles stiffened at the sight of her. Her face was red and blustery with anxiety. Billy Bob had his arms around her shoulders, patting her gently, and it took everything inside my not to run down to them and beat him and her about the head with my bare fists.

What's wrong with you? Pay attention to the handsome dude next you and forget Billy Bob.

"Are you okay?" Dominic asked. "Maybe we should get out of here. I'll walk you back to the courthouse."

I reined in my anger and…jealousy. Damn it! I had no reason to be jealous. Billy Bob could court whomever he wanted. After all, I was on a kinda-date with Dominic.

I patted his forearm that crossed my upper chest, but I didn't take my eyes off Billy Bob. "You're right. We should go." As if he sensed me watching, Billy Bob's gaze snapped to mine. His lip curled in a snarl as he glared at me.

I glared right back. Then, maturely, I stuck out my tongue, spun out of Dominic's arms and headed down the block to Twelfth Street with Dominic on my heels. Before I could turn left to cross to the courthouse, a strong hand gripped me by the arm and spun me around.

"What are you doing here?" Billy Bob demanded. I'd never seen such a look of pure rage on his face before. I could see the hint of his wolf slipping into his eyes.

After a stunned moment, I responded with a confused and slightly angry, "What?"

He growled as he drew closer, both his hands now on my upper arms, his claws digging into my skin. Not enough to hurt, but enough to warn me he was serious.

"Get your hands off her," Dominic said.

"Leave," Billy Bob told him. "Leave now."

To Dominic's grit, he stood his ground. "I think you're the one who should leave, Doctor Smith."

So they knew each other? Of course, they did. Billy Bob had been working with the council since their arrival and Dominic was one of the Arkansas delegates.

Please don't kill him. Please don't kill him. I recited the mantra in my head, silently pleading with Billy Bob to let it go. "I'm okay, Dominic. You have business at the courthouse, so you should go."

"I…Are you sure?"

"Yes," I said, afraid to look away from the scary-acting werewolf. "I'll be fine."

"If you're sure."

"Go!" Billy Bob commanded.

I jerked out of his grip. "Christ on a cracker, Doc! Will you calm down?" I thumped his solid, puffed out chest with the back of my hand. "Just chill a second." I turned to Dominic. "I really am okay. You have business, so you should go do it."

"Are we still on for lunch Sunday?" he asked, glaring at Billy Bob and not looking at me.

"Yes," I told him. "I'll meet you at one o'clock at the Blonde Bear Cafe."

Unexpectedly, he relaxed and gave me a dazzling smile. He brought my hand to his lips and kissed my fingers. "It's a date."

The rumble coming from Billy Bob made my stomach flip.

"Okay." I took my hand back. "You better get on now. I'll see you later."

He gave Billy Bob one last look. "Count on it."

Oh, hell. I rolled my eyes as I turned around to face the angry lycan.

"What game are you playing, Chavvah?"

"I'm not playing any game. What the hell is wrong with you?"

His jaw worked back and forth. I shivered remembering this morning's kiss. Wowza. I'd never seen this man so enraged, and frankly, it made his stupid ass even sexier. Ack!

"Why are you down here on the Riverfront?" he asked.

I shook the giant giraffe at him, its knobby horns flopping forward with its head. "Is this an interrogation? Because the last time I checked you hadn't been deputized." It pissed me off that he was making this so personal. There was another murder. It could be a friend or a neighbor for all we knew, and he wanted to know what I was doing? How about if we figured out what the killer was doing instead?

"I don't want—" He bit off whatever word he was going to say when foxy Bethany caught up to us.

"I've been looking everywhere for you," she said. Her long, thick black eyelashes fluttered.

Billy Bob replaced his angry expression with a placid look of congeniality. "I'm right here." He gritted out a smile.

I ground my teeth with irritation. He must have noticed a change in my demeanor because he looked smug for a second. "Bethany, can you give Ms. Trimmel and me a moment to converse? It won't take but a tick."

Her damsel in distress act faltered for a moment, and I could see the cunning in her eyes as she examined me up and down. Then she filled her face with innocence again and tilted her head back to look at him. "Of course," she said. She tapped his chin. "Just don't take too long, you hear?"

"Oh, I hear," he said.

When she walked away, he didn't seem near as angry anymore. Crap. He liked Bethany. I pissed him off, and she calmed him down. This was just more proof of how un-right we were for each other, even if he had almost managed to practically give me an orgasm with just a kiss. Okay. Not just a kiss. Damn, why did kissing Billy Bob have to feel so freaking good?

"Did you hear about Ed?"

Well, at least he wasn't asking me what the hell I was doing anymore. "Yes. I was with Ruth when Ed came home."

"It's good." He nodded, his silver hair falling over his shoulders. "It's good it wasn't him."

I nodded my agreement. A woman walked past us, a jar of chipped sassafras in her hand. "Do you still have the body at your clinic?" I wanted to tell him about what I smelled, see if the new victim carried the same scent.

"Yes," he said, his expression wary. He took my hand. "Chavvah, promise me you'll be careful."

His concern ruffled my calm exterior. "I will," I said. "You too."

I don't know who was more surprised when he leaned down and gently pressed his lips to mine. A zinging tingle zipped up and down my spine, and my sexy bits begged for mercy. My hands pressed against his chest and curled against his pecs. The man tasted like an exotic dessert.

I didn't want to, but my eyes closed of their own bidding as I leaned into the kiss, my lips parting for him in an invitation to claim. He pulled back, staring down at me, his eyes blazing with intensity.

"I have to go," he said. His voice was rough and thick. "The body…"

"Yes, yes," I panted. "The body." I stepped back to put distance between us. "I…I have to go too." I turned on my heel, big cumbersome giraffe in hand, and walked away as fast as my jelly legs would carry me.

Damn it. I hadn't told him about the sassafras!

CHAPTER 7

THE RESTAURANT WAS DARK, and I left the lights off as I hurried up the steps to the apartment. Surprisingly, my leg had stopped aching since Billy Bob's kiss. Now that I thought about it, I'd had fewer aches after our morning make-out session as well. I knew lycanthrope saliva had healing properties, but I'd never had it orally before. I smiled and then cursed myself for being a stupid, crushy girl.

Right now, Billy Bob was comforting Bethany Hilliard. She absolutely threw off the "mine" vibes when she'd joined us, and Billy Bob had done nothing to discourage her. Did I really want to be on his list of women pining for him? Nope. Not even a little bit. So why did my hoo-ha jump for joy every time I thought about him. It was a goddamn betrayal!

Someone knocked at the apartment door, and I pretty near peed myself. Had I left the restaurant unlocked when I came in? I thought I'd locked the door.

How could I be so dumb? Had I left it unlocked last night? What the hell was wrong with me? It was like my brain had moved and hadn't bothered to leave a forwarding address.

The knock sounded again. "Chavvah?"

A wash of relief flooded me as I recognized Babe's voice. I opened the door. "How did you get into the restaurant?"

He tucked his chin, surprised at my greeting. He held up his keys. "I used these."

"Oh, thank heavens. The door was locked. I thought I was losing my mind for a moment."

He walked past me into the living room. "Too late for that."

I backhanded his shoulder. "Don't be such a pain in the ass."

"It's my official job as the youngest Trimmel." He brought me in for a brotherly hug and then gave me a smacking kiss on the cheek. "You all right?"

"Nope. But I'm dealing."

Babe nodded. "Sheriff Taylor released the crime scene, and Roger Messer is doing the cleanup for us."

"He's good people." Roger was Blondina's husband. Before coming to Peculiar, he and Blondina had owned a cleaning company. They'd been integrators at the time. When she got pregnant with Selena, they'd decided to raise her in a therian community. They'd wanted her to be proud of her heritage. Totally the opposite of my parents.

Babe wore a tailored blue suit, and his normally messy hair had been styled neatly. Also, he'd managed a shave. This Babe was a stark contrast to the Babe I'd grown up with. I was absurdly proud that my baby bro was the mayor, and I marveled at how much he'd matured over the past year.

I examined his expression with the experience of an older sister. "What is it?"

He hemmed and hawed for a couple of seconds, toed the shag carpet with his fancy shoes, then chewed the inside of his cheek before finally meeting my gaze. "I think you should think about going to Kansas City for a couple of days."

My hackles rose. "No." There was no way I would give Mom and Dad the satisfaction by running to them in a crisis.

"You are just as stubborn as Sunny."

"Did you ask her to go stay with our parents, too?"

His ears turned red, and he managed chagrinned. "Yes."

"And yet, you're still breathing."

"Barely." Babel sat down on the chocolate brown couch, a new purchase since I'd moved in. The cushions were big, like clouds of pillows, and so much better than the ugly old 70s furniture my older brother Judah had settled on. Though, if I could have Judah back, I'd have gladly lived with his poor taste in couches. "Sunny's psychic ability hasn't been right since Jude was born, and with all these strangers in town, it would be dangerous for people to find out she's human." He slanted a look at me. "The last thing I need is for my two favorite women to get any more involved in these murders."

"Hey! It's not my fault someone put a corpse out back of the restaurant."

"I know that. But it wasn't an accident, either."

Sudden realization flooded me. "You think someone was trying to send a message to us? That maybe someone knows Sunny isn't a therian?"

"I don't know. It's unlikely. But I want to keep my wife and my sister as far away from this investigation as possible."

I plopped next to him on the couch and took his hand. "You won't get any argument from me. But I don't need Mommy and Daddy to protect me, either."

"Well, at least stay with us. I have to spend a lot of time in town, and it would make me feel better if you are with Sunny and Jude when I can't be," he told me. "The Tri-Council just had an emergency meeting because of the deaths." He shook his head. "It's too late to move the Jubilee to another town, but they are considering closing off the bridge to keep more folks from coming in—or from leaving. And they want an accounting for everyone in town and our surrounding territory. That's over a thousand of our citizens, and probably another three or four hundred therians from the surrounding states. It's going to be a logistics nightmare."

He looked tired. Babe was in his mid-twenties, but the responsibility of being mayor of our town was taking a weighty toll. I still couldn't believe that my die-hard integrator brother was in charge of a shifter community. If someone had told me two years ago that we both would have made our homes in Peculiar, and that he would be married to my best friend, I'd have laughed until I cried.

I nudged his shoulder with mine. "You know I'd do anything for you and Sunny, except run off to the city, of course. We're going to make it through this, like always."

He nudged me back. "I know. I've got to get back to the courthouse. The Tri-Council should be wrapping up their business."

"How come you weren't in on this meeting?"

"They wanted members only for the first hour."

"Hmm."

"There's no conspiracies, sis. It's standard business. They want to figure out what they really want before they ask. Frankly, it will save a lot of debate."

"Okay." I shrugged. "Have fun with your grown-up stuff." I winked at him, and he kissed my cheek before jumping up from the couch.

At the door, he turned and gave me one last look. "Don't take any risks, Chavvah. I'd really appreciate it if you and Sunny would keep out of the investigation. At least as much as possible. I can't risk you. Either of you."

"I promise I'll avoid danger at every turn. And I'll try to keep Sunny from digging too much."

He put his index finger up. I stood up and walked over to him. I touched the tip of his finger with mine. "Heart-light swear," I said.

He smiled. "Thanks. You're the best."

"Damn straight. Now get the hell out."

He held up his hands. "Going."

I closed the apartment door and locked it. Just in case. I was paranoid. Not without cause, but I hated feeling scared and vulnerable.

After a quick shower, I pulled my hair back into a ponytail. Another knock on the door had me jumping out of my skin. Who now?

"Babe?" I asked. I really needed to get a door with a peephole.

"It's me. Sunny."

Well, shitty-shitty bang-bang. I unlocked the door and opened it. "Why are you here and not home?"

"I need a reason?" With her big boobs, she appeared perkier than usual. I was looking forward to when she finally weaned Jude off the milk train. Those taters were distracting.

"You shouldn't be here, Sunny. Especially not with all that blood around."

"I didn't go out back. No worries." She waved off my concern and strolled in taking the exact spot on the couch where Babe had been sitting. She sighed unhappily. "Besides, I haven't had a vision in weeks. I used to wish they'd go away, and now... I can't believe I miss them."

I smirked and sat down next to her. "Why are you here?"

Her lower lip jutted into a pout. "You're a terrible best friend."

"Am not."

"Are so."

"Uh-unh."

"Uh-huh."

"Are we going to be sticking out our tongues soon and calling each other doo-dee heads?"

"Maybe." She giggled.

I giggled too. Not something I normally did, but Sunny knew how to bring out the girl in me. She hugged me and, as usual, it made me feel better. "You give the best hugs, honey."

"I know." I could hear the smile in her voice. When she leaned back, she frowned at me. "Are you okay, Chav? I am really worried about you. You should be packed and at the cabin, not sitting alone in this apartment. What if the killer came back?"

"If he'd wanted me dead, he had every opportunity last night." I shivered as goose bumps rose on my arms. "I had my earphones in, so I didn't hear anything. Nothing at all."

"Oh, Chav. That so awful."

"And I smelled something strange, and I keep forgetting to tell…well, anyone, about it."

"Tell me."

"It smelled like sassafras. I thought it might be root beer last night, but it had a more pungently spicy aroma than soda. And at Ruth's this morning, she had a jar on her shelf."

"So happy it wasn't Ed," Sunny said. Her relief echoed my own.

"Gosh, yes. Me too."

Sunny put her hand on mine, and I took it, glad for the comfort.

"Anyways, it turns out one of the street vendors is using it as a prize or selling it or something. Ruth's middle boy, Butch, brought it home from Riverfront Street. I was going to try and find where he got it from, but then…"

"The other body floated in."

"Exactly!" I pulled at the hem of my tank top with my free hand. "I tried to tell Billy Bob."

"Billy Bob, huh?" Sunny smirked.

"Don't look at me like that."

"And what were you doing with Billy Bob down on Riverfront?"

"Nothing," I said. "I was down there with one of the Tri-Council guys—"

"Which one?"

"Dominic Tartan."

"Day-yam!" Sunny whistled. "That is one fine, fine specimen of a man." She wiggled her brows.

"Shut up." I laughed. "Anyhow, Billy Bob was with an *important* delegate."

"Jacob Lowry?"

Jacob Lowry was the Lowry brothers' father and the president of the Tri-Council.

"Nope. Not him. I'm talking about the she-fox from Arkansas."

"Oh." She made her mouth a small "o" shape then spit out her next word. "Bethany."

"That'd be her." I couldn't keep the snarl off my lips.

"She is truly awful."

I threw up my hands then. "Thank you! She is a terrible person. I don't know why the doc is so fascinated with her." I bobbed my head. "Oh, wait. I know. It's because she's stunning and petite." I glanced at Sunny. "Besides, I think he has a thing for blondes."

Sunny's smile was soft and gentle, not teasing. She pulled my ponytail over my shoulder and fanned it over the right side of my chest. "Chavvah, you have the most attractive dark, caramel-colored hair, and it's all natural, doll. If I had your hair color, I'd never dye my hair again. And as to stunning, ten Bethanys couldn't hold a candle to one you."

"As my BFF, you have to say these things."

"I don't know why you can't see what everyone else does." She put her hand in her lap. "Darling. Billy Bob Smith is in love with you."

I choked on my own breath. "Oh, no, he isn't!"

Sunny gave me an exasperated, thin-lipped smile. "For a smart girl, you really are clueless."

"Did you have a vision or something?"

"Nothing like that."

I can't even say how much her lack of vision disappointed me. If it was something she saw in a psychic episode, then I might possibly believe. Did it really matter? "I'm not in love with him."

Sunny snorted. "You hear that?" She tilted her ear out.

"What?" I hadn't heard anything. "What do you hear?"

"My bullshit meter." She shook her head. "It's clanging like a fire engine on its way to a five-alarmer." She stood up. "Get your shit together, woman. You're coming home with me, and that's that."

"Okay." At least it was better than going back to Billy Bob's. I couldn't trust myself around that man. And no, I wasn't in love with him.

"I'll follow you out to the cabin," said Sunny. "Jo Jo is babysitting Jude, and I promised him I wouldn't take too long."

"Are you still worried about him?" Jude was going on five-months-old, and he'd passed six full moons without a single shift. Therian babies aged slower than human babies, so Jude was about the size of a three-month-old human infant now. Even so, they usually shifted under the first full moon after their births, but with hybrid therians, it could take up to a year, and on the rare occasion, they might be born without the ability. In those cases, the child was usually put up for adoption in the human world. It was dangerous to keep a non-shifting child in a shifter home, especially on the full moons.

"Babe keeps telling me I shouldn't worry, but I'm worried. What if he doesn't ever shift? What if he's as human as I am?"

"At least, he'll have you. You won't have to give him up like other shifter families."

Her mouth went slack, and her eyes widened. "It's too horrible, Chav. I can't believe therianthropes give up their babies if they don't transform."

"It's out of love, Sunny."

"I know," she said. "Enough of this depressing as shit talk. Go get ready."

"Fine," I said. "Give me ten minutes, and I'll be ready to go."

She tapped her watch. "Tick tock."

"Bossy bitch."

"Yep." She smiled. "Hurry up. These milk jugs are going to explode soon."

I made a high-pitched noise and watched, satisfied, as her smile faltered and she looked down at her leaking boobs. She grabbed a pillow from the sofa and threw it at my backside. I squealed and jumped as it brushed passed me.

Another knock startled us both, and I realized I hadn't shut the door when Sunny arrived. A tall man, burly chested with dark hair and an unruly beard stood in the doorway. "Sorry, ladies. Didn't mean to sneak up on you," Roger Messer said.

"It's okay, Roger."

"I'm done with the cleanup."

"That's so great of you," Sunny said, holding my favorite throw blanket over her wet shirt.

I cringed and made a mental note to throw it in the wash as soon as possible. "If you send us a bill—"

Roger shook his head. "This one's on Blondina and me. You gals have been through enough, God knows."

He reached into his utility apron. "Found this near the corner of your porch. Figured it was some kind of spice y'all used in the kitchen." He held out a twisted root about three inches in diameter. I could smell it now. Faintly. It was sassafras.

I took the item from him. When Sunny moved in for a better look, a foreboding welled inside me, and I instinctively stopped her. I don't know why I didn't want her to touch it.

"What's wrong, Chav?"

"I don't know." I examined the twisted twigs. The dark wood had been woven into an eight-point star.

"You should let me try and get a vision."

"No." I pressed it between my palms and held it away from her. "It stupid, but humor me. I think there's something wrong with this...thing. I think I should take it to...Oh Lord."

Sunny's face brightened. "You're going to talk to a certain hunka-hunka werewolf, aren't you? Ooooo. Chavvah and Billy Bob sitting in a—"

I flicked her in the nose.

"Ow!" She rubbed the tip.

Roger Messer cleared his throat. He wasn't smiling, but his eyes crinkled with humor. "I'll finish getting my stuff out and get on home now."

"Tell Blondina hello for us, and thanks so much for your help."

Sunny, still holding my throw over her jugs, gave Roger her most charming smile. "You are appreciated."

Roger smiled then. "See you all later."

I shut the door after him and turned to Sunny. "Well, we better get out to the cabin. I want to do Internet research before I decide to do anything. This token could be absolutely nothing. It's probably a homemade child's toy." It pulsed in my hand as if it were a living thing, and I nearly dropped it.

"Fine." Sunny's narrowed gaze followed me as I went to pack fresh clothes. "But we're going to talk about this more when we get to the cabin."

"You got it," I promised, gripping the twig star harder. "We'll try and figure it out together." Whoops. So much for my promise to Babe to keep our noses out of the investigation.

CHAPTER 8

"I CAN'T BELIEVE YOU CALLED RUTH."

"She's super awesome at this kind of thing, Chav. I just happened to mention the twisty toy, and she already had a few ideas." The doorbell rang. "That's her!" Sunny was excited about the new mystery, and I chalked it up to BMS, Bored Mommy Syndrome.

After hugs all around, we all sat at the kitchen table with steaming mugs of coffee and slices of blackberry cobbler with ice cream that Ruth brought. As I bit into the deliciously tart cobbler, still warm from the oven, I reassessed her added value to the clue party.

"Chav doesn't want us touching it for some reason," Sunny said when I held up the star.

Ruth leaned forward. Her lips pursed as she carefully kept her hands on her mug and examined the sassafras.

"It's an eight-point star," she said.

"I have ten fingers, so I managed to count that high." I picked my foot off the ground. "With my toes, I can go as high as twenty."

Ruth laughed. "Smart-aleck."

"Do the eight points mean something?"

"Yes," she said. "If I remember right, it has some kind of meaning in Christianity. Something about redemption."

I grabbed up my phone and pushed the microphone icon. "Find eight-point star," I said into the base of the phone. A bunch of search results popped up, but I clicked on the first one. "Uh oh."

"What?" Sunny and Ruth were both scooting closer in their chairs.

"It means gazillions of things to a gazillion different people."

"You're exaggerating," Ruth said.

I showed her the screen. "But not by much."

Sunny slid her finger up my phone. "There's the Christian reference. It means redemption or regeneration. There some stuff in here about astrology. And some witchy stuff."

"Do you really think the killer left this last night?" Ruth asked.

"I'm not sure of anything." Other than I was more confused than ever. Was it a coincidence? Had someone from the fair dropped this outside the restaurant?

Maybe it had been in one of the trash bags that burst when I tripped over the body. Why was I making such a big deal about a scent and an eight-point star?

A phone rang. It was Sunny's. "Hey, Babe," she said when she answered. "Yes. All right."

I could hear him ask her to put him on speakerphone once she confirmed I was there.

"Chav, they identified the first body. We're still working on the identity of the second one."

My stomach lurched. "Who was it?" Please don't let it be someone I like. I knew it wasn't someone I loved. They'd all been accounted for.

"Mike Wares."

"Mike?" I gripped the star again. He'd been the prime suspect when the sheriff had thought Ed was the victim. "I can't believe it." He'd been a volatile man, but he certainly hadn't earned this fate.

"Nobody deserves to die that way," agreed Babe. "I'm nearly home. I'll see y'all in a few minutes."

He ended the call. We all looked at each other in shock.

"Oh, damn," Ruth said. "Mike is Blondina's half-brother. They didn't always get along, but family is family."

"Half-brother?" I asked.

"Yes." Ruth shook her head. "They both have the same father, a grizzly shifter who'd been one of the town's founders—Albert Ware. Blondina's mom was Albert's first wife. She was a bear shifter. Albert left his wife for Mike's mother. She was a raccoon shifter."

"So he's a mix like Jo Jo?" Sunny leaned forward with rapt interest. "I had no idea."

Sunny leaned forward. "Does the child usually change into the father's animal? Like Jo Jo being a coyote and Mike, a bear?"

"A lot of times that's the case, but not every case. Sometimes a child will get his or her mother's form. And, while it doesn't happen often, every once in a great while we'll get a child who can't shift at all." She said the last part with remorse. "It's the chance two of our kind take when they cross species. I've never heard of any child of a mixed mating being able to shift into more than one animal. I'm pretty sure it's impossible."

I'd already known this, but for Sunny, as she waited for baby Jude to have his first shift, I could tell it hit a nerve. She still felt like an outsider, and she wanted her son to be a real part of the community.

Which is why it didn't surprise me when she deftly changed the subject. "So, Chav. What's going on with you and this Dominic-dude?"

Ruth leaned forward, elbows on the table and chin on her fists. "Oooo-ooo. Do tell me more."

I rolled my eyes. "There's nothing to tell."

"He has dreamy eyes," Sunny said.

"I'll tell Babe you think so."

She scrunched her nose and patted my knee. "You do that." Without missing a beat, she turned the conversation to Ruth. "Those Lowry boys are cute as well."

"There has been an influx of handsome, available men in our town with this Jubilee." Ruth looked meaningfully at me. "A single girl could really have her pick. Especially one as a pretty as our Chavvie here."

"I'm not shopping for a husband."

"You should be," Sunny said. "We could be having babies together!"

"Ruth can have babies with you."

"After seven children, I think my ovaries are retired."

Sunny gave her a pleading look.

"For good," Ruth reiterated.

Sunny huffed. "Fine."

It dawned on me then just what my bestie was saying. "Are you pregnant again?"

She smiled coyly. "I've taken two home tests that say I am."

"Oh my God!" Ruth squealed. She and I both jumped up with Sunny and all three of us danced our glee in a group hug.

"I'm home," Babe shouted from the living room. He walked into the kitchen and caught us in our celebratory clutch. "Everything okay?"

Sunny gave Ruth and me a *don't-say-a-word* glare. "Everything's great, Babe."

"Really great," I said too enthusiastically. I winced when Sunny pinched me.

"I better get home," Ruth said. "Gotta get supper on. The price you pay when you decide to have a herd of kids. Ow!" She gave Sunny a dirty look. My BFF didn't look at all sorry for pinching Ruth, too. "Thanks for having me over." Quietly, she mouthed to us. "Call me."

I nodded. "Thanks for the pie."

"There's pie?" Babe asked.

Sunny laughed. "I'll get you a plate and a fork."

* * * *

"Aaa-ieeeee!" A scream from Sunny had Babel and me scrambling toward the bathroom. Babe, carrying baby Jude, practically kicked down the door to get inside.

What we saw defies actual words. Sunny, naked as the day she was born, had one foot in her tub all the way to the far side and the other foot out on the tile floor, effectively doing the splits and barely keeping upright.

"Don't just stand there," she shouted. "Every time I try to stand, my foot slips farther in. I'm about to crotch-land on the edge of the bathtub if someone doesn't help me!"

Babe thrust a cooing, oblivious Jude into my arms and rescued his wife by easily lifting her up and out of the foamy tub water.

"What happened?" I asked, gurgling with repressed laughter.

Babe grabbed the nearest towel from a rack and wrapped Sunny up.

"Not funny," she said, shaking her finger at me.

"This ranks right up there with scrubbing your face off," I pointed out.

"Shut up. This wasn't my fault." Her cheeks turned pink. "It's been a long time since I've had a pedicure, so I went to Dolly's this morning, and the day has been stressful, so I thought a eucalyptus bubble bath was in order, especially with you and Babe taking care of Jude. I just wanted to pamper myself for a minute."

"And that explains doing the splits how?"

"My foot is really smooth, Chav. So is the tub. Add soap, and voila, I'm ready to be the next circus act." She glared at me. "I swear to God if you tell a soul…"

"Would I do that?"

"Yes! I'm still trying to live down the allergic reaction I had to the hair depilatory that I used on my lip."

"I only told Ruth. Maybe Blondina."

She snapped her fingers then slipped as her wet feet skittered on the tile. Babe caught her by the arms and hauled her up. "Not. A. Word," she threatened.

"Spoil sport."

"I think it's time I got my wife to bed," Babe said, smartly staying out of the banter.

"I am exhausted," Sunny said. "Jude hasn't been sleeping well, which means I haven't been sleeping well."

And she was voluntarily having another baby? No, thank you. I hoped she told Babe soon. I was no good with secrets. Babe took Jude back, and my hand went inside my sweat pants pocket to the wooden star. I hadn't told him about it. Or the sheriff. Hell, other than Sunny and Ruth, no one knew about it. Well, Roger, of course, because he found it, but why did I want to keep it to myself? I hadn't let anyone touch it since I took it from Roger. Guilt niggled its ugly way through me, but really, the damn thing could have just been a trinket. It didn't have to have anything to do with the murder. Right? I stroked it again, enjoying the textures against my fingertips.

Sheesh. Was I going to start hacking up fur balls and calling it *my precious*?

I hoped not.

By eleven p.m., Sunny and Babe were in their bedroom, but I couldn't sleep. I could hear the TV on in their room, some cop drama I think. They had it turned down low, and I could hear Baby Jude snoring away over their baby monitor. That kid was going to need a good ear, nose, and throat doctor when he got older. I tossed and turned on the couch. Even with the lack of sleep the night before, I couldn't shut off my brain. The star wouldn't let me rest, and the slightly sweet and spicy smell kept it at the forefront of my mind. The smell had been stronger last night. Had it faded that much in such a short time or had the smell come from the victim? Gosh. Poor Mike. I didn't know him well, but given his exchange with Ed, I understood how he'd gotten his reputation. Still, he was a part of my community, and now he was dead. It made me sad and sick to think about. Another thought occurred to me: Would Sheriff Taylor question Ed about Mike's death? Maybe he was a suspect now that he wasn't a victim. But Ed had a pretty good alibi.

Who else had been murdered? The image of the bloated skinned body in the lake sent a shiver right through me. I wondered if anyone had found an eight-pointed sassafras star with the other corpse.

Remorse assailed me. I really should've told the Sheriff about the star. And I had promised Babe to stay out of the investigation. Still, I couldn't stop wondering about the second victim.

Screw it. I'd go to Billy Bob's and see if I could get info about the second body. And I'd show him the star. Maybe his woo-woo magic had some explanation for it. Maybe it really was just a spice and meant nothing at all.

I didn't change out of my sweats and oversized T-shirt. I didn't want the doc to think I was trying to impress him. I slid on my flip-flops and grabbed my car keys. I was not going to think about our kiss or how much I'd wanted to seal the deal.

Why had he kissed me? I almost felt better when I knew there was never going to be anything between us. No matter what else happened, we'd always have those two toe-curling, soul-lifting, body-clenching kisses.

Damn you, Billy Bob Smith, and your stupid, stupid lips.

I bumped a lamp stand on my way to the door. It wobbled, making a thump, thump, thump sound. "You okay out there?" Babe shouted from the bedroom.

Shit. "Fine," I told him. "Just getting a drink of water." I felt a small boost of triumph when I managed to get out the door without making another sound. I used my key to lock the door—carefully.

Chavvah Stealth Trimmel, at your service.

I hoped like hell my car didn't wake Babe or Sunny when I started it up. It was a nice two-door sedan, a quiet model, so I wasn't too worried as I pulled out onto the rural road. I played through everything I would do when I got to Billy Bob's place. Business only. I'd show him the root, ask about the body, and be on my way.

So what if it was almost midnight?

Crap. I should have worn a bra. And combed my hair. It was still up in a ragtag ponytail, and several long strands had fallen out of the rubber band and flew wildly around my face. I could have rolled up the windows and turned on the air conditioner, but I liked the feel of the air on my skin, especially on such a warm night.

When I pulled into Billy Bob's drive, I noticed a soft glow coming from his sweat lodge. Was he performing a ritual? I'll admit, even though I didn't buy into his kind of hokum, I was fascinated by his beliefs. Besides, Sunny had told me how he was practically naked when he had taken her to the sweat lodge after rescuing her from her car accident. Which is why I turned the car lights off and coasted up the hill, trying hard not to stir up the gravel, and why I found myself at a full stop less than a hundred yards from the sweat lodge.

Treacherous ovaries! They really wanted to see a mostly naked Billy Bob. Or all naked. That worked too. Did he pray and chant as he danced around a fire? It dawned on me, for a guy I'd known for almost three years, I really knew very little about him.

I rolled down the window and slid out of the car. I didn't want to take a chance his wolf hearing would pick up the door opening and closing. I let my coyote surface so I could see through her eyes. It allowed me to avoid clumps of dry grass and loose rocks that would give me away. I made it all the way to the front of the sweat lodge without once making any noise. My klutzy-self, still less clumsy than Sunny, wanted to high five my sneaky self, but that would have defeated the whole purpose of being quiet in the first place.

Chapter 9

I HEARD SOFT CHANTING. I gently pulled back a leather flap at the entrance and peeked inside.

Two gray eyes stared back at me from less than a foot away.

I yelped and stumbled back, but not before a quick hand reached through the opening and pulled me inside.

"What are you doing here, Chavvah?"

"I … uh." His pure masculinity was an aphrodisiac.

"Are you in pain?"

Yes. Yes, I am. Pain from wanting you hardcore. I noticed he wore nothing but a loincloth, and his body was covered in swirls of light and dark clay that covered all of his skin, even his face.

He leaned in close and sniffed me. Honest to heavens, took a long-ass whiff of my scent. "You don't smell like you're in pain." He offered a feral grin. "You smell like desire."

"Don't tell me I smell like desire." He really threw me off-kilter. I wasn't even making sense to myself. Two could play the sniffing insult game. I leaned forward and inhaled his scent. "You smell like..." *Bergamot and spice and everything nice.* "...like dirt."

He moved in so close I felt his breath on my face. "Smell again."

Oh, Lord. He smelled earthy, and musky, and orange-y, and wowza, sexy as hell. The juju he threw my way made my heart do somersaults, turned my knees to mush, and created a flood of pure want that made my panties wet.

I groaned. He growled. He'd been doing that a lot lately. "What do you want from me?"

His eyes glowed with intensity, his wolf so near the surface I could smell his fur. "Everything," he said.

My body burned, and while the sweat lodge was hot, I knew Billy Bob was the main source of my heat. I wanted him, but God how I didn't want to want him. "We can't," I panted because I'd stopped breathing like a normal person a few seconds earlier. "It won't work."

"Why do you have to be so damn stubborn?" The exasperation on his face matched my frustration.

"We're too different. We come from different worlds." Literally. Lycanthropes and therianthropes, while both shifters, had very different origins.

"You are not as different as you think, little sister." The tall form of the man who'd been in my room the night before, the one whose voice I'd been hearing for a year, appeared near the fire at the center of the circular room.

A scream escaped me. Billy Bob held onto me so I couldn't flee. "That's him. He's the one who tried to get me last night."

"I only wanted to talk." The guy's tone was calm and reassuring, which made me panic more.

"You don't sneak into someone's bedroom and scare the shit out of them just so you can have a conversation." I tried to yank out of Billy Bob's grasp. "Let me go!"

"Chavvah. You need to listen."

"The hell I do!"

He shook me then, not hard, just enough to get my attention. Before I could protest, he kissed me, and let me tell you, that shut me up but good.

When he'd pretty much macked the resistance out of me, he eased up. "This is not a man."

"I can see him right there."

"And what do you see?"

"A big, tall guy."

"Look again."

The man's face and body, like the night before, was all shadow. Even in the firelight, I couldn't make out any distinguishing features. It was as if he were made of smoke. "What is this?"

"He is known by many names."

"You may call me Brother Wolf," the shadowy figure said. "We are old friends, Chavvah."

"I don't understand."

"He is of the spirit realm, another plane of existence. He is a guide." Billy Bob stared intently into my eyes. "More specifically, he is my guide."

"I am not exclusively yours, brother."

Irritation passed over Billy Bob's expression. "I realize that, Brother Wolf. What I don't understand is why you've revealed yourself to Chavvah?"

"Because you asked me to."

Billy Bob looked as confused as I felt. He turned, finally letting me go, and faced the shadow man. "I don't understand."

"When she was taken, brother. You prayed for intervention on her behalf."

"You knew where she was?" Anger made his words crisp. "You knew the whole time? Why didn't you tell me?"

"Time. Place. These mean nothing to me. I could no more tell you where she was than tell you where she is now. Or you for that matter. I do not see the world as you do. I do not see with mortal eyes."

"You could have told me she was okay."

"But she wasn't. I knew telling you would bring you pain." The shadow pointed to me, and I could feel his hand on my shoulder. "You are strong, sister. Strong and brave. Then and now. Do not fear your destiny." His form turned to Billy Bob. "You must be honest, brother. You must tell her the truth. She needs to accept who she is. She needs to accept what she must become." And with those ominous words, the shadow dissolved against the sweat lodge wall.

When I was able to speak, I looked at Billy Bob, and asked, "What the fuck?"

"You are no longer only two-natured, Chavvah."

"I don't know what you mean."

"Last night, when you shifted…"

"Yes?"

"It wasn't into a coyote."

I had felt the transformation. I ran on four paws. I hadn't hallucinated being in my animal form. "Now I'm really confused."

"You changed into a wolf. An elegant brown and white timber wolf. I knew there was something about you, almost from the moment we met, but I never dreamed." He shook his head. "I've dreamed of you, but I never dreamed I would find you."

"Who do you think I am?" I couldn't believe what he was saying.

"A spirit talker, like myself. A kindred wolf." His eyes grew glassy with emotion. "A mate." He touched my cheek. "My mate."

Everything he said was too unreal to believe. It was as if he were speaking in a foreign language. "I better call the UN, because I think I need an interpreter."

He huffed angrily then yanked me into his embrace. I opened my mouth to protest, but he silenced me with his lips. Unable to help myself, because, well, Billy Bob made my libido want to take charge, I leaned into him, my fingers threading through his hair as his tongue swept inside my mouth. The euphoria of his kiss was better than any anti-anxiety pill, and I rode the high that came in the form of this stubborn werewolf.

He stopped kissing me with the same suddenness in which he'd started. "Did you understand that, or do I need to call that interpreter?"

"Uhm," I licked my lips and tasted a mixture of clay and spice. "I think I get the gist." I looked down at my T-shirt. It was sprinkled with dried mud flakes from Billy Bob's body. "You're really covered in that stuff."

He shook his head, and within in seconds, he turned into a wolf. His gray eyes blinked up at me in a very serious manner. He was large, at least twice the size of a coyote male. I chewed my lower lip as the air around him began to shimmer. In a few more seconds, Billy Bob was standing in front of me again, his body free of dried clay, his loincloth on the ground, and his rigid erection very impressive.

"Better?"

"Uh…huh." I licked my lips. He was a large man in every way, and frankly, I was worried I wouldn't be able to handle him. But man-oh-man, did I want to find out.

"Chavvah." His intense expression was dark with an edge of angry heat. "If you walk away right now, I won't pursue you. We are mates, but you must be willing to join with me."

My ears burned as irritation replaced my desire. "I'm just supposed to fall into your arms or fall out of your life. Is that what you're saying? You're one arrogant man, Billy Bob Smith."

His expression shifted to one of amusement. "I've been pursuing you for almost a year now, Chavvah. I don't know how else to show how much I want you."

"Well, you can start by actually telling me. Have you tried that? Like ever?" He opened his mouth then snapped it shut. "Exactly!" I said. "Unlike Sunny, I'm not a freaking psychic or a mind reader. How am I supposed to know how you feel if you don't say so?"

"I usually don't have to spell it out."

"Usually?" A vision of Bethany Hilliard fawning all over him popped into my head. "Usually! I'm not one of your bimbos, either. I have standards, and those standards don't include standing in line behind a bunch of women to get my Billy Bob fix. Just because I'm in love with you doesn't mean I'm going to fall down on my knees and thank my lucky stars you want me. I hate to tell you this, buddy, but you aren't the only man in town who finds me attractive."

"What did you say?"

"You aren't the only one who thinks I'm cute!"

"Before that."

"I'm not going stand in line behind your parade of—"

"After that." His voice was low and dangerous. He was up on me again, close enough that the heat of his chest warmed my cheeks.

"I…" What had I said? I'd been so caught up in my angry rant. There was stuff about falling at his feet, and… oh, shoot. "I have no idea what you're talking about."

"You said you love me."

"I love a lot of people." I started counting on my fingers. "There's Babe, Sunny, Jude, Jo Jo, my parents sometimes…"

"And me."

I couldn't meet his gaze, so instead I rolled my eyes.

He cupped my chin and tilted my face back.

Reluctantly, I looked him in the eye.

"And me, Chavvah."

The way he stared at me, as if I were an oasis at the end of a long desert walk, made it hard to deny him anything, even the words he so badly wanted to hear from me. "Why?" I asked. "Why are you putting me through this?"

"Don't you know?" He dipped his head and brushed my lips with his. "I'm in love with you, too."

"I…" Wow, this was not the way I had thought this night would turn out. Not at all. "How can I believe you?"

He stepped back, his exasperation apparent. "Why are you so difficult?" He threw up his arms.

It dawned on me that I never see Billy Bob mad or angry or irritated with anyone but me. The realization made me smile.

"What?" he asked. "Why are you smiling?"

I shook my head and giggled. Damn it.

"And now you're laughing."

"You really have no idea, do you?" I stripped my shirt over my head and exposed my naked breasts to him.

"What are you doing?" His tone was suspicious.

I pushed my sweatpants down, after giving only a moment's consideration as to whether I'd shaved recently or not. "Well," I said to him.

"Well, what?" His erection was pretty adamant now as he stared at my body with a hungry gaze.

I held my hands out to my sides, palms up in invitation. "Are you going to stand there all night, or are you going to come get me?"

The low, rumbly groan that tore from his lips as he closed the distance between us made my thighs quiver.

Billy Bob lifted me from the fur-covered floor. I wrapped my legs around his waist, feeling his thickness slide against me. He moaned as his fingers tangled in my hair and he buried his face in the crook of my neck. He nipped and licked my skin, teasing me, as he tugged on my ponytail hard enough to expose my throat. I felt his teeth clamp down over my carotid.

The heat of his breath, the slight pain of his bite, it made me feel heady with need. I whimpered, rubbing myself against his abdomen. "Oh, Billy Bob," I muttered. "God, I want you."

His mouth sought mine, and we merged in a dance of lips, teeth, and tongues. It was as if I could feel him pouring his passion into me through my mouth. I fought to give him as good as he was getting, and when he backed me up against the lodge wall support, pulled my legs up higher, and entered me, I cried out at the sheer relief I felt having him so deep inside me.

His grunts and moans matched my own as sweat poured down our bodies. I grasped him tightly, loving the friction of my breasts against his slick chest as he thrust into me over and over.

"Yes!" I made the word a demand. It had been so long since I'd held anyone, and never a man who made me feel one iota of the emotion or pleasure I felt right now. The burning edges of climax warmed my body and heat pulsed through my groin. So when he shouted something unintelligible and guttural, I exploded around him. Pleasure ripped through me like a chainsaw, just as brutal and just as messy.

Billy Bob groaned as his grip on me tightened. His thrusting quickened until he gave one final stroke that he held until he spent himself inside me. I collapsed against his shoulder, my sweaty body slipping as his grip loosened. Gently, he withdrew from me and set me down. My jelly legs could barely hold me up, so I was grateful he kept his arms wrapped around me.

He put his forehead against mine, his eyes closed. "That wasn't how I imagined our first time."

"Oh," I said, unable to keep the lazy smile off my face. "And how did you imagine it, because frankly, if it gets more exciting than that I might need a better health insurance plan."

He laughed now and met my gaze. "You are an unpredictable woman, Chavvah Trimmel."

"Is that what I am?"

His smile faded and the lines around his eyes deepened. "I am in love with you. I have been for a very long time. I apologize that I did not make my intentions clear to you from the moment I realized you were the one."

"And when did you realize?"

He smiled. "It was shortly after you'd started to mend your broken femur." He meant my thigh bone. "I wanted to help you walk, and you wanted to do it on your own."

I nodded, my forehead rubbing against his. "I remember that."

"You said, "I'm stronger than I look," and I thought, you are stronger than anyone I've ever met. You kept yourself from shifting while those men did terrible things to you. You kept your will to live after three weeks of starvation and torture. And when you came home, you fought to heal on your own terms. I'd never seen anyone so stubborn and fierce." He kissed me again, his touch tender and sweet. "And I knew."

I couldn't keep the grin off my face. "You have weird taste in women."

"You're telling me."

"Doc," I said.

"Yes?" He kissed me again.

I kissed him back and traced his face with my fingers. I still found it hard to believe I was touching him, that he was in love with me, and that he wanted to be mine and mine alone. I loved the way his heart beat so hard I could feel it in my own chest, the way his breath cooled my hot, sweaty skin, and I loved the way he looked at me like a woman worthy of worship. "All right," I admitted. "I am in love with you too."

"I'm glad," he said with a happy sigh. "So very glad."

"So…" I squirreled my mouth sideways. "What's all the spirit talker nonsense, and how can you explain to me how I'm turning into a wolf?"

"How about if we go up to the house and shower first, then I'll explain what I can?"

A shower with Billy Bob sounded just about perfect. "Deal."

He swept me off my feet, literally, holding me in the cradle of his arms. "You're slippery."

"Don't let me go," I said, embarrassed when a giggle slipped out.

"I don't plan to." His gaze narrowed on me. "Ever."

* * * *

The shower had been just as hot as the sweat lodge, and I wasn't talking about the water. I never knew how dirty getting clean could be, but I was ready to roll in mud if it would get me back there quicker. Billy Bob kept touching me, even after, as if he thought I'd disappear if we weren't anchored to each other. Had I really been so awful that he thought I was going to bolt the second I got a chance to really think about the ramifications of being a lycanthrope's mate?

Holy shit. A lycanthrope's mate. How the hell did I explain that to my parents? And, crap, I'd never hear the end of it from Sunny. That bitch was never going to let up with all the I-told-you-sos and the happiness talk. What was I getting myself into?

He kissed me, and I swear to God I felt as if he were filling me up like an empty gas tank on payday.

He smoothed back my hair, still wet from our shower. "Let's get dressed. We'll talk in the kitchen," Billy Bob said. "If we stay in the bedroom, I can't be responsible for my actions." Billy Bob's hand trailed down my back, making me shiver in all the right places.

Whatever I was getting into, I knew for certain, I didn't want out.

While he ran to get my clothes out of the sweat lodge, I hurried to the car and retrieved the star.

By the time I dressed and got into the kitchen, Billy Bob had tea and sandwiches ready. I was starving now—lycanthropes had big appetites.

I sat across from him and said, "Okay, spill."

"Brother Wolf is an animal spirit. He began talking to me after my grandfather died. He taught me the ways of healing the soul. I went to med school because my calling to heal was so strong, I wanted to be able to help people in all ways."

His altruism made me feel inadequate. "My only goal was to open a restaurant with my best friend so we could hang out all day together. I'm a total asshole compared to you."

"True," he said without a hint of humor.

"Hey!"

"I'm kidding. Brother Wolf was my grandfather's spirit guide. He was a shaman for our people." Saying "our people" pained him.

"Other lycanthropes?" I realized I knew nothing about the way wolves lived. Other than Billy Bob, I'd never met anyone of his kind. "Did you live in a pack?"

"Of a sort," he said. "We live in groups, but it's not like fiction books where there is one alpha for each pack."

"It rarely is." I laughed. "I've seen what stories get made up about therians. Hell, most writers don't even get the language right." I drew him in close to me and relished the feel of his hands on my back as he wrapped me in his arms. "You mean you aren't going to go all he-wolf-alpha on me? Wait. You already did." I matched his wicked grin with one of my own. "Okay. Tell me about Brother Wolf."

"He's a guardian." He shook his head. "Of sorts. He can't intervene with the mortal plane. He can only interact. The fact that he chose you…"

"Because you prayed for me." And he'd done that before he loved me. It really did say a lot about Billy Bob as a man.

"I wish I—"

"We can't turn back time," I interrupted. When he didn't say anything, I asked, "We can't turn back time, right?"

"No. We can't turn back time, but if I could, I would kill them all. I would do it with my bare hands."

"You're a healer, not a killer. I like that about you. I don't want you to change because you're angry on my behalf."

"But these killers, whoever they are, I'm afraid, Chavvah. I'm afraid for you. It's why I want you here."

"So you can babysit me?"

"Yes."

His bluntness threw me. "I'm not a baby, Doc. Bad things happen. If anyone knows it's true, it's me. But I can't hide from evil. It finds us no matter where we are. I won't pretend to understand everything going on with me. These changes. You say I turned into a wolf, and I believe you. You're stubborn, egotistical, and a general pain in my ass, but you're not a liar."

"You have the sweetest way with words."

"You say this voice in my head that showed up as some dark shadowy figure is a spirit guide named Brother Wolf, I'll allow it. We both saw him and heard him, which means unless you were burning drugs in that sweat lodge fire pit—" I tucked my chin for a second then tilted my head back to glare at him. "You didn't put hallucinogens in the fire did you? That shit is still illegal in this state."

"No, Chavvah. No drugs," he said, then muttered, "not this time, anyhow."

I let it go. "So we can discount mass hysteria. The stuff about me being a spirit walker."

"Spirit-talker."

"Whatever. Can we push pause on all this mystical hoodoo voodoo monkey magic until we can figure out whose killing people around here? This is making my brain hurt. I wish the Jubilee had never come to town."

His face held a look of disappointment. "If that's what you wish."

"I wish. Definitely."

"Okay."

Speaking of the killer. "Having sex with you wasn't the reason I drove out here tonight."

"No?"

"Oh, don't look hurt. You were a pleasant bonus."

"That's a consolation."

"Sheesh."

"Why did you come tonight, Chavvah?"

Every time he said my name, my heart skipped a beat. I think he knew it too. "I want to get a look at the second body. Maybe the first one as well. And I wanted to show you something."

He dropped his gaze to my T-shirt.

"Ha, ha. No, I mean something else. But first, did you smell sassafras on them?"

Billy Bob blinked. "Yes," he said.

"On the second guy as well?"

"Yes." He tapped his chin. "And little else, other than blood and meat. There's been a lot of it going around the fair. I didn't think much of it."

"Could the killer have used it to mask his own scent?"

"It's not a bad deduction. I didn't smell anyone else on the bodies. Just their own stench and the light smell of sassafras."

I pulled the star from my sweatpants' pocket and held it out for him to see. "Roger Messer found this while he was cleaning the restaurant for me. It feels important."

"What is it?" When he reached for it, I pulled it back. He didn't try to touch it again.

"An eight-point star," I told him. I turned it in my hand, my fingers tracing the twisted edges.

"It could be something to do with religion or rituals, or it could be some kid's trinket," he said.

I clasped the star in my fist, and I swear I felt it pulse again. "I can't shake the feeling that it has to do with the killings. Do you know who the second victim is?"

"Jerard Blackwell."

"Blackwell?" I'd heard that name, but where? "Jerard? As in, Jerry? A woman was asking about him this morning at the police station. A chick named Willy Boden."

Billy Bob groaned. "I've met her."

I grinned. "She's feisty, for sure. Anyhow, she was looking for this guy. Said he'd gone missing." Once again, I was relieved that the victim wasn't someone I knew and loved. "Was it the same as the first one?"

"Yes. He'd been skinned while still alive, his throat cut after."

I shuddered. "It takes a sick, sick mind to come up with some heinous crap like that."

"I've seen worse." He closed his eyes for a moment as if shaking a memory. "I was a war medic during Vietnam."

I met his gaze, and I could see he meant it. Even though he didn't look it, Billy Bob had to be close to sixty-years-old. Undoubtedly, he'd seen a lot over the years.

"Come sit with me in the living room. I don't want to be apart from you."

I followed him to the couch, and we cuddled on it like two love-struck teenagers. I touched his cheek with my non-star clutching hand. "I'm sorry for your pain. I'd take it from you if I could."

"My father never believed his dad could really talk to spirits, so when I began my journey as a spirit talker, he made my life in our community miserable. I joined the military as a way to escape my family."

"Seriously?"

He smiled sadly and stroked my cheek. "I figured I'd rather face an enemy that I didn't have personal or blood ties with. I walked over one hundred miles to the nearest recruiting station. A week later I was sent off to basic training. I became a combat medic because I wanted to heal people. To help."

"And that's why you became a doctor?"

"Yes, when I returned to the states, I made my mind up to the go to medical school." His silvery hair spilled forward, tickling my face as he kissed my forehead. "There were times when I thought Brother Wolf had abandoned me, and it took me many years to get to a place where I really trusted him." He shook his head and chuckled. "Now I find out that you can talk to him any time you want."

"I'm sorry."

"Don't be. Am I envious? Yes. Am I happy for you? Yes. I am glad Brother Wolf is with you. I'd spare you all this horror if you'd let me, but knowing our spirit guardian is with you, at least gives me some comfort."

"I'm glad too, but I hope you know I wouldn't thank you for treating me as if I couldn't handle it."

"I know." He sighed. "It's two in the morning. We should try to get some sleep. Are you going to open the restaurant tomorrow?"

"Today, you mean." I made a mental note to text Sunny before going to bed to let her know I was okay. Ugh. I did not want to deal with her innuendoes, especially now that they would all be true!

He smiled.

"Yes, oh, wait. It's Sunday." The last three days had melded into one awful blur. "We'd planned to open for breakfast only." I flinched as another thought occurred to me. "I have a lunch date with Dominic Tartan."

Billy Bob's lip curled, and his body began to vibrate with agitation. "No."

"He might have some insight into the victim. He'd seemed to know the ex-girlfriend, Willy Boden, when she came into the police station. I think I should keep the date."

"No."

I patted his chest. "I've never seen you act this way, Doc. Don't you trust me?"

"Fine," he said, instantly changing his demeanor. "I guess I'll keep my lunch date with Bethany Hilliard as well. She might know something about Blackwell too."

"If she touches you, I might have to kill her," I said.

"Same goes for Tartan," he said without humor. The blazing intensity in which he stared at me made my heart race and my palms sweat.

"Oh God," I groaned as a highly developed sense of possession overtook me, and I leaped up and wrapped my legs around him. I let him kiss me until I was light-headed, and when he said, "I'm taking you to bed," I said, "Take me right here, and then take me to bed."

The delicious roar that tore from his chest when he bent me over the coffee table made me cry out in triumph. After two spectacular orgasms, he took me to bed, where he made love to me, slower, gentler, as he whispered how much he loved me over and over until I cried.

CHAPTER 10

I'D NEVER BEEN IN BILLY BOB'S cooler. In here, he kept things that needed refrigeration, like certain medications, burn treatments, and, apparently, dead bodies. He kept the room at thirty-six degrees. In other words, ass-crack cold. It was five in the morning, and he finally agreed to let me see the corpses.

He had three body drawers. Frankly, I thought it was odd he even had one, but as the only medical doctor in a therian community, I guess he had to be ready for anything. Seeing a skinned person in the stark, fluorescent light took away any mystery that might have remained for me. Without shock to protect me, I could see the muscle striations, the bones where the killer had cut too deeply into the flesh as he filleted the skin. I sniffed, sifting through the myriad of aromas on the corpse. There was the expected blood and meat, the sassafras, which seemed to cover his entire body, not just in his mouth, but there were other things as well.

"Do you notice the burnt smell?"

"Yes," Billy Bob said. "I believe it is thyme."

"The herb?"

"Some cultures believe it purifies the soul. Not that this is part of a ritual, but…"

"It all feels ritualistic, like what I've seen on some of the crime dramas on TV." I thought of the star in my pocket. "Whoever is doing this, I don't think they're done."

"I agree."

"What can you tell me about Blackwell?"

"A thirty-six-year-old therian, born and raised in Oklahoma, moved to Kansas to join a community when he was twenty-two. His father was bear, his mother coyote."

"So he was mixed?"

"Yes."

"Mike Wares was mixed too. Bear and Raccoon."

"Hmmm." Billy Bob tapped his chin. "Probably just a coincidence. Two doesn't make a pattern."

With my armchair degree in criminology thanks to the Investigation Discovery channel, I thought the killer was too confident for these to be his first murders. He displayed both bodies at places where the possibility of getting caught was high. "I bet if the sheriff looked, he'd find similar murders somewhere. And with people in from Kansas and Arkansas, he should start inquiring there as well as Missouri." I crossed my arms and stared at a metal shelf across the room as the smell of disinfectant began to overtake all others. "I'd read in an article that there are serial killers all over the place, and most never get caught because they don't have any real motive other than to kill." I glanced back at the bodies. "These poor guys probably never even saw it coming."

"I've sent off blood samples for analysis. I think they were drugged, or at least paralyzed while the perpetrator did this to them. I don't know how, but I think they might have been forced to partially shift."

I cringed as I remembered the way the hunter's guards had tormented me, trying to force me to shift. There were so many sick fucks in the world. Billy Bob put his arm around me and kissed my temple. "Seen enough?"

"Yes. More than." I rubbed my upper arms. "I better get back into town. Jo Jo and Sunny are opening."

"I'll tell the Sheriff about the sassafras. You really should give the star to him—it's probably evidence."

I nodded, even though I had no intention of handing over the star. I didn't know why, but it needed to stay with me.

"Sunny is going to be unbearable," I said. My *not-to-worry* text sent at 2 a.m. didn't mention Billy Bob, but after the night I spent with the doc, she would know! And not because she was psychic. My BFF had a gift for reading me as easily as a Doctor Seuss book.

"Tell Tartan hello for me," he said.

"Tell Bethany to go to hell for me," I said back.

He smiled. "We'll meet up at three. Your apartment?"

"It's a plan." I rose on my tiptoes and kissed him. I'd meant it to be chaste, but he encircled me in his arms and commanded me with his lips, conquering me where I stood.

When he finally let me go, he said, "Remember. I'll kill him."

I shivered all the way down to my toes as he and his fine ass walked out of the cooler in a grand exit. Until I realized he'd left me alone with bodies. Son-of-a-bitch!

I swore under my breath and fled the room with all the grace of a deer on ice.

* * * *

Sunny's Outlook was slow for breakfast. After we'd closed the day before and news of the murders had gotten around, we apparently declined in popularity for Jubilee attendees. Granted, the body had been left outside, but still—it wasn't exactly an appetizing image to associate with a restaurant.

The bridge out of town had been manned with guards because the town council and the Tri-State council had voted to close off the town, nobody in or out until the murderer was found.

The sheriff's office was busy tracking down everyone in town both residents and visitors to take their information. Sunny volunteered us to help man the intake booths to get initial information from folks in the afternoon. I wanted to smack her, but I couldn't very well say, "No," now. I told her I couldn't do it until after four. I had lunch with Dom, and no way was I missing my meet-up with Billy Bob at three…not that I told Sunny about it. As a matter of principle, I had avoided proximity with my bestie all morning.

I wasn't ready to answer questions about what was going on with me and the doc, especially since it involved more than just my heart. Was I really turning into a lycanthrope? How was that even possible? Yes, there was wolf blood in my family dating back several generations, but Ruth had been right the night before when she'd talked about how therians were always only one animal, no matter their parentage. Jo Jo was a coyote like his dad, not a mountain lion like his mom. This was how our biology worked. So how could this be happening to me? Billy Bob was a lot of things, but he wasn't a liar. If he said I turned into a timber wolf, no matter how incredulous, I believed him.

It is my doing, sister, the voice in my head said. I dropped the plate I was washing.

Now that I knew the voice was real, I replied back. "How? And for fuck's sake, why?"

I can only communicate with my children. Coyotes are not mine.

"I thought I was your sister."

You are my sister, my daughter, my mother. Where I am, we are all.

"That's some real philosophical shit there, Brother Wolf."

I could almost feel his smile. *Good, then we are accepted.*

"How did you manage to make me into a lycan?"

It was already in your blood, little wolf. I just called to the part of you that I knew would answer.

"That explains everything." Not really. I still didn't understand everything about this spirit talking, but I thought it strange that I could talk to Brother Wolf while doing the dishes, while Billy Bob needed a sweat lodge and a whole bunch of ritual.

You did not call to me, sister. I called to you. The summoning is mine.

I wanted to get it, but I didn't. "So, you find me. Is that what you're saying?"

In order to find you, you have to be lost. You are important to me, child. If you need me, I will come.

"Uh, thanks." I felt his presence fade. I rinsed the dishes I'd just scrubbed and contemplated the fact that I'd was talking to a spirit in the *aether*, a type of otherworld plane of existence. At least that's how Billy Bob had explained it. And not only was I talking to him, but he'd also turned me into one of his own. I wanted to be mad about it, but without Brother Wolf, I would have never made it out of that hunters' lodge alive. I would have shifted. I know that now. He'd kept me strong. Sane.

Well, as sane as I could be after everything I'd been through. Belatedly, I sent up a silent thank you to my spiritual guardian. Mom and Dad were going to be seriously freaked out when they found out that not only was I dating a wolf, I was turning into one, and I was talking to *the* wolf spirit.

Oh well. They'd get over it or they wouldn't.

"I'll finish up," Sunny said as she peeked around the door to the kitchen. "It's almost noon. I say we close up for the rest of the day. I don't think we're going to get more customers. Besides, you better get going for your date with Dominic." She made kissy faces, and I flipped her the bird.

"Love you too," she said.

I unplugged the drains in the triple sinks and hung up my apron. After a quick check of my hair and makeup, I headed out for Blonde Bear Cafe.

Main Street was quiet compared to the prior three days. The murders had definitely put a damper on the festivities. However, Blondina's restaurant was packed. Even horrified, people needed to eat. Dominic was seated at a table in the far corner of the room. His expression was darkly contemplative. He was doing something with his phone, but it was hard to tell what. He could have been texting, searching the Internet, checking out his social media, or playing a game of Angry Turds. When he set his phone down, he looked up and saw me. The darkness ebbed in his expression as his frown turned into a very charming smile. It gave me a warm fuzzy to know he was glad to see me. *Bad Chavvah.*

He waved at me. I waved back and headed to the table.

Before I could sit down, Blondina Messer came over with a tall glass of ice tea for me. She was a tall, curvy woman, who always reminded me of Flo from Mel's Diner, a TV show my parents used to watch. She set the tea on the table. Its perfume made me gag. Sassafras. Ugh.

"I'm sorry, Chav." Blondina blinked. "I thought you'd like it. Elton Brown got some great sassafras wood in for his furniture shop, and he's chipped the bark for tea and potpourri. It tastes really good. I swear."

"Elton's the one selling all this sassafras?"

"Yes," she said. "He's made some fine-looking pieces with it as well. Some of his best work."

The eight-point star was burning a hole in my windbreaker pocket. I resisted the urge to reach for it.

Dominic stood up and came around my side of the table and pulled put my chair. "Speaking of fine-looking," he said. "You are looking rather fine this afternoon, Ms. Trimmel."

This close he smelled like cinnamon buns. I had to resist the urge to lean in and inhale deeply. No man should smell like dessert…or maybe all men should. I thought about Billy Bob, and I smiled. He *was* dessert.

I took the offered seat. "Thank you, Mr. Tartan."

Blondina picked up the iced tea. "I'll go get you some regular, hon."

Two tables over, Wilhelmina aka "Willy" Boden sat with Hans Fisk, Randy and Chance Lowry, and a large man with dark brown hair and eyes. I could tell he was older, but like I said before, with shifters, it was too hard to tell. The shape of his jaw and his angular nose looked enough like the twins for me to suss out he was probably their father. I leaned across the table and asked quietly, "Is that Tri-Council President Lowry?"

Billy Bob had told me Lowry owned a big chain called Beaver Locksmiths. Their slogan was, "Call us if you're in a jam." I supposed it was a play on a log jam. Har-har.

He smiled. "Yes, it is. Would you like to meet him?"

I brightened. "Sure." It would mean being formally introduced to Willy, the dead guy's girlfriend. After all, she was probably on the suspect list. She had fought with him before his disappearance, and she might say something that would help me put the whole mystery into context.

"After we order, we'll make a quick appearance."

"Awesome."

He had his chin tucked in and his eyes on the menu, and when he turned his gaze up to me, he did it in such a way that if I hadn't been completely smitten with Billy

Bob, I would have been asking, his place or mine. But, as it was...

"Isn't that your friend from yesterday?" He pointed toward the door.

My back was to the door, so I swiveled my upper body to see whom he indicated. I nearly swallowed my tongue as—speak of the devil—Billy Bob came in with the very sexy and bitchy Bethany Hilliard. My ears burned, and a swift and severe jealousy made me shake. I stuck my hand into my pocket and stroked the star like a stress stone.

Billy Bob's gaze met mine, and I could see the tension in the fine lines at the corner of his eyes. Had he brought Bethany here to make me jealous, or to keep an eye on me because he was jealous? The way we were both vibrating, I had a feeling it might be both. Billy Bob's black jeans hugged his ass and his thighs in all the right places. The azure blue button-down shirt he wore made his gray eyes pop with vibrancy. My girly heart squealed for more of him, but my woman brain kept me in check.

"Are you okay?" Dom asked.

"Fine," I said, unable to tear my gaze away from Billy Bob.

Why was this happening to me? I felt as if I had no control over my reactions when he was in the same room with me. Twenty seconds earlier I'd been a charming, logical, intelligent adult but seeing Billy Bob with Bethany had made me feel like a thirteen-year-old watching another girl flirt with her boyfriend. In other words, I was about to go all middle-school-rumble-in-the-playground on Bethany's tight booty.

Dom put his hand over mine, and I barely felt his touch. My mouth dried out completely when I saw Billy Bob's lips peel back ferociously. Crap! I wanted to jump his bones right in the middle of the restaurant.

Dom's hand withdrew. "Chavvah."

"Uh-hmm," I said, still looking at my werewolf mate.

"Chavvah," he said more urgently.

I dragged my gaze away from Billy Bob to look at Dom. "Yes?" I bit my lower lip.

"If you were already seeing someone, you could've told me." He didn't sound angry. Maybe disappointed, but not pissed.

Call me petty. I would have been pissed. "I'm sorry, Dom." I held up my hands. "It literally just happened. And believe me, no one is more surprised than I am."

"When nature calls," he said, his tone slightly wistful. "I understand."

"I'd still like to get lunch if you want." I smiled at him. "You're a nice man, Dom. I'd like to be friends."

"I think your boyfriend would rather see me skinned alive." He winced. "Sorry. Poor choice of words."

"So you know then." I paused as Blondina dropped off a new glass of ice tea. "About me finding the body." Tripping over it, really.

"Yeah," he said. "Terrible. Just terrible."

"Mike wasn't a peach by any means, but he didn't deserve that kind of death."

"No one does," Dominic agreed.

Since he'd sort of brought up the killings, I pressed forward. "The second victim is Jerard Blackwell. Is that Willy's boyfriend?"

Dom lips thinned. "Yes. Poor bastard."

"Agreed. Really awful."

"He was a delegate from Kansas." He shook his head. "I hate to be a dick about the dead, but the guy was an ass."

"It must be awful for Willy and her brother Hans." I still couldn't get a read on the broody, moody Hans Fisk.

Dom's mouth tugged up at the corner. "Willy will bounce back. She's not the kind of woman to let flies gather."

Oh, right. Randy Lowry had told me Willy and Dom had a history. "Did she break up with you?"

He looked at me, his stare assessing. "Not exactly."

"I didn't mean to bring up a sore subject."

"I've been over her a long time. She might shift into a mountain lion, but she can be a raging hellcat."

His summation took her to the top of my suspect list. But why would she have killed Mike? And why leave him behind Sunny's Outlook? And why the hell would she skin them? "What did her brother think of Jerry?"

"I don't think Hans liked Jerry, but I also don't think it had much to do with his relationship with Willy. Hans and Jerry were business partners in a modular home scheme. I heard through the grapevine they had a falling out." He glanced at Willy's table then back to me. "Hans is a general contractor. Worked his way up from journeyman to build his business."

I could feel Billy Bob's eyes burning a hole in my back. I tried to ignore him and his date. It was next to impossible. I couldn't stop looking. I was super proud of myself for not running over and yanking every blonde hair from Bethany's perky head.

I am the model of civility and restraint.

"Did Mike Wares have any enemies?" Dom asked.

It was a fair question, considering I'd just grilled him about Jerry Blackwell. "There were lots of people in town he rubbed the wrong way, but I don't know about enemies. Frankly, I'd be sick to think anyone I knew and liked could have anything to do with the killings."

"Was there anything odd about the body when you found it?"

Tiny alarm bells rang in my head. This was an unusual question to ask. Was Dom making small talk, was he fishing for answers for the council, or did he know more about these murders than he should? I decided to tell a half-truth. "I smelled sassafras. Billy Bob said Blackwell's body had a similar scent."

Dom steepled his fingers, his pale green eyes darkening with interest. "Really? Anything else?"

You mean, like the eight-point star in my windbreaker? I raised a brow. "No. At least nothing I saw that night." Again, a half-truth. I hadn't known about the star at that time.

He frowned.

Dakota Thompson, Ruth's oldest daughter, stopped at our table. She wore an apron and held a pad and pen in her hands. "Can I get your order?"

"I'll take the salmon," Dom said. "Slightly rare."

"Sides?"

"Pilaf and broccoli."

"That's a healthy meal," I said. "I'll take the double bacon cheeseburger with Blonde Bear Secret sauce and all the fixings." I handed her our menus. "Oh, rare on the burger and an order of fries and onion rings for sides."

Her brown eyes twinkled as she fixed her gaze on me. "You got it, Chav."

Dom laughed. "I may have to sneak some of your fries."

I heard a growl behind me that warmed my entire body. "Probably not a good idea."

Dom shook his head. "Noted." He stood up. "Let's get you introduced to President Lowry."

As we made our way over, Willy Boden noticed Dominic and her expression soured. For a woman who just lost a boyfriend, she didn't seem all that upset, but I suppose everyone grieves in his or her own way. Her brother seemed to be perpetually sour. I wondered if anything brought him pleasure.

Maybe skinning therians and slitting their throats, I thought morbidly.

Randy Lowry, or at least I assumed so since he was always smiling and his identical twin sat like a lump, jumped up from his seat. "Hey, Dom." He shook Dominic's hand. "And how nice of you to bring us such attractive scenery to go along with our delicious meals." He looked at me as if he wanted to make a meal out of me.

I laughed. "You're a funny man, Randy."

He glanced down at his brother. "She can already tell us apart."

Chance didn't bother to respond.

The fiery redhead stood up next. She held out her hand to me and gave mine a firm, confident shake. "I'm Willy Boden."

"Chavvah Trimmel."

"Nice to meet you, Chavvah." She clutched her hands. "This is so awful. Both killings."

"I'm sorry for your loss," I said.

"Poor Jerry. Goddamn maniac getting him, of all things." She threw up her hands. "And skinning him." Her raised voice attracted stares from the other diners.

"Calm down, Willy. We don't want to get everyone riled up," the large, older man said.

"People should be riled up," Willy said. "It's been a security nightmare, for shit's sake. The town folk should be in their homes, doors locked, and refusing to leave until this goddamn week is over. And the council members and the tourists should be doing the same thing."

Hans glowered. "You go too far, Wilhelmina. Sit down."

"When I put you in charge of my ass, I'll send out an official memo. Until then, fuck off."

I couldn't hide my smile. I liked Willy Boden, which meant I hoped like hell she had nothing to do with the murders. I turned to the older man. "You must be President Lowry. It's so nice to meet you."

He gave me a tight-lipped smile. "You own that deli down the street, Sunny's Outreach?"

He made it sound like a halfway house. "Outlook," I said. "Sunny's Outlook." I tried hard not to look irritated. "We specialize in vegetarian meals. We'll be supplying food for your big meeting tomorrow."

"Good, good," he said with bluster. "Nice town you have here. Too bad about the trouble. It's been an…inconvenience."

Jacob Lowry made serial killing sound like a flat tire or a broken washer. I was certain Mike Wares and Jerard Blackwell wouldn't have agreed.

"Good grief." Hans Fisk stood up. "I'm going back to the Hilltop Hotel. I can't take any more of this."

When he raised his hand as if to fend off any arguments, the sleeve of his shirt slid up revealing a tattoo. A star tattoo. "That's nice," I blurted out.

"What are you on about?" Hans asked.

"Your tattoo," I said, then idiotically added, "I've been thinking about getting one myself. Can I see yours?"

"No," he replied, his voice flat. "Willy, text me if this ban on leaving town is lifted."

"Wait up," Chance said as he got up from the table. "I'll walk out with you."

Hans stalked out of the restaurant with Chance on his heels and a scowl on his face.

"Well, I certainly didn't mean to offend him," I said to Willy.

"Don't mind Hans. He was born dramatic," she said.

We both laughed.

Randy Lowry leaned in close, wiggled his brows and said, "I have a tattoo I'd love to show you."

About that time, a wall of werewolf butted up against my back. I could smell the bergamot and spice, along with possessive jealousy and anger.

I raised my brows and smiled. *Me likey.*

"Dr. Smith," Jacob Lowry said. "Nice to see you." He gestured just past me. "Did you enjoy lunch, Bethany?"

I shifted my eyes just enough to catch her in my peripheral vision. She was standing near Billy Bob, but not touching him. Good thing too, otherwise there would have been a schoolyard throw down in Blondina's restaurant, and I didn't want to create extra work for my friend.

"The food and the company are just divine," she said.

The sound of her voice made my teeth hurt. *I will be a grown up. I will be a grown up.*

"Billy Bob has been such a sweetheart, showing me around town."

Sweetheart had become extremely quiet.

I will not look. I will not look.

Bethany continued. "I think I could really learn to love this place…given the right incentive."

I could smell her cloying rose and berry perfume as she moved closer. *Be calm, sister.*

Shut the hell up, Brother Wolf.

As you wish.

Great. I'd gone and hurt my spirit guardian's feelings.

When Bethany's hand touched my arm after she looped it past Billy Bob's elbow. I spun on my heel and faced them both. Billy Bob looked as if he'd swallowed a bug. Bethany looked like the cat that ate the canary.

Quickly, he removed her arm, but all too late. I leaped up on him with an agility I hadn't felt since my recovery, wrapping my legs around his waist as his hands found their way to my back. I growled, snapping at Bethany once, before turning my heated glare upon my handsome werewolf's face.

He did not look surprised or upset or even chagrinned. He looked…ready to go. Billy Bob yanked my head down by my hair until my lips were on his, and he crushed me with a kiss that had me whimpering with need. I fisted his silver curls with the same ferocity, delving my tongue between his lips as I staked my claim. *My man*! I thought. *My fucking man.*

When the overwhelming desire to take possession of him ebbed a tiny bit, I couldn't help but notice the entire restaurant had gone completely silent. I reluctantly withdrew from the kiss and slowly pivoted my gaze to take in all the gaping town folk and Jubilee attendees who'd witnessed my brain snapping in two.

I bit my lower lip, my legs still wrapped around Billy Bob's waist, and glanced down at him. He had a big, goofy grin on his face and a dazed look in his eyes.

No help there.

Suddenly, someone shouted, "Oh my God!"

My BFF Sunny stood just inside the door with Ruth Thompson, and they were both squealing like teenage girls who'd gotten a glimpse of their favorite boy band.

I carefully climbed down Billy Bob, hoping my feet wouldn't fail me when they hit the floor. I gave Bethany a hard stare, pointed my finger right at her, and said, "There will never be the kind of incentive you want to keep you in town." I looked up at Billy Bob, who grinned like a jackal, and said with great emphasis, "Never."

Her lower lips quivered as I brushed past her on my way to the door. The questions on both Ruth's and Sunny's faces almost had me turning back around and running in the opposite direction. The grilling I would get from those two ladies when they got me alone was going to be a shitshow of epic proportions.

"Not now," I told them. "Later." Much, much later. As I walked out the door of the restaurant, I realized I hadn't eaten lunch. Hell, I hadn't even said goodbye to Dom. I was a lousy date.

"Get a room," Delbert Johnson said, as he walked past me into the Blonde Bear. He laughed.

"How in the hell did you…"

He held up his cell phone and played a video of me making out with the doc. Freaking technology! Nothing was sacred.

In my insane jealousy, I'd managed to out my relationship with Billy Bob to the whole entire town. The video would come back to haunt me over and over again. I'd have to put up with kissy faces and knowing looks from every customer who walked into the restaurant. I wondered if I could "call in stupid." If there were a trial, I was certain a plea of not guilty by mental defect would be upheld. I'd lost my damned mind, and I lost it in front of everybody.

Why was this happening to me?

I went to Sunny's Outlook, shaken by my sudden claiming and abandoning my mate. I was all twisted up with joy and surprise and horror. I shut the door behind me.

It suddenly registered that I'd entered the main dining room without using my key. Why the hell would Sunny leave the restaurant unlocked?

I headed for the light switch, but as I threaded my way through the tables, I smelled the tang of animal musk and the sweetness of sassafras.

Shit. I spun and headed for the exit, but a sharp sting in my neck slowed my pace. I screamed as terror filled me like a hive of buzzing, angry bees. A hand slapped over my mouth, and I felt dizzy, warm…light headed. Whoever it was, had doped me. No, no, no! In a few seconds, I felt floaty and dreamy.

My heart cried out for my mate, for Billy Bob.

Then there was nothing but endless dark.

CHAPTER 11

I HEARD A VOICE, BUT IT was far away, distorted. I opened my eyes, but I realized I'd been blindfolded. As I reached full consciousness, I heard two voices, but I didn't recognize either of them.

Something heavy hit against my leg. I wanted to cry out, but my voice didn't work. I couldn't see, I couldn't talk, and I couldn't move. I could only hear. Panic consumed me. I was trapped. Frozen inside my own body. Terror filled me, but I beat back that familiar foe. *Think, Chavvah. Think!*

I remembered Billy Bob talking about how he thought the first two victims had been paralyzed. Is that what was happening to me? I heard the clang of metal against metal, the crunch of feet on gravel, and the roar of a diesel engine. The uneven surface under my back dug into my skin. I had to be in the back of someone's truck. That narrowed down the suspect pool by about two people. Everyone in town had trucks and so did most of the Jubilee group.

My adrenaline spiked as panic set in—an appropriate response to being kidnapped by an evil, therian-killing bastard. It took a scary confidence to snatch someone up in broad daylight. Damn. I was tired of being a victim!

I tried to scream for help, but again, I couldn't make my mouth work. Nothing worked.

The truck started moving. The rough ride bounced me around, and the tarp over the top of me rubbed against my skin. I wondered if it was still light outside. Was anyone missing me yet? Billy Bob and I were supposed to meet at three this afternoon. Sunny and Ruth expected me for volunteer work at four. Was it close to those times? Past them?

I focused on calming myself. After my ordeal last year, Sunny had bought me a crap-ton of self-help books. I didn't read them all, but one had talked about anxiety and panic, and it had said that when "flight or fight" is triggered in someone, it could make it hard to think rationally. Irrational thought was dangerous. Bad decisions were made when people panicked. Keeping calm when you're paralyzed, was not an easy feat. I was failing miserably. It dawned on me my spirit friend had been conspicuously absent.

Brother Wolf! If ever I needed a guardian it was now.

Little sister, he said. *I am here.*

I need help. I've been drugged and taken, and I can't move. I can't do anything. I hated feeling so damn helpless. So weak. *You have to let Billy Bob know what's happening to me.*

I can't speak to him the way I speak to you.

Why not? The tiny bit of Zen I'd found was disappearing rapidly.

Why does the wind blow?

Don't be a dick.

I am not trying to be a semblance of male genitalia.

My irritation did for me what nothing else could. It pushed back at the fear. *How long have I been gone?*

Seconds. Hours. Days. Years. I have no concept of time.

I was beginning to regret calling for him. *Do you know who has me? Who is the killer?*

I can only see you.

Again, not helpful. My frustration level rose like a hot balloon on a cold day. *What good are you?*

I am here.

If my eyes hadn't been paralyzed, I would have rolled them. Hadn't Brother Wolf said he'd brought my wolf to the surface and that he'd somehow manipulated my genetics to change me so that he could speak to me? Could he change my body in other ways?

Can you help me flush the drugs from my system?

He remained silent for a moment. When he finally spoke, he said, *Maybe.*

That one little word gave me hope. *How?*

You must focus on your creatures. It will take both wolf and coyote to burn out the poison. Even then, I'm not sure it is possible. Your coyote has gone dormant.

What? How?

Two nights ago, you embraced the wolf. Coyote is a jealous creature.

Illogically, I was offended. *How do I unoffend my freaking biology?*

You must embrace both beasts as part of you. You must be both.

Fundamentally, I understood what he was asking, but Ruth had been right when she said that we had one form and one form only. How in the hell was I going to be both?

It is in you, Chavvah Trimmel. You have been both. Your coyote is still there. It just needs to be found again.

Won't the wolf run off then?

No. I will not allow it.

Well, la-di-da. I hated to admit it, but once again, the voice in my head, the one I now knew as Brother Wolf, had given me hope. I concentrated on my coyote, searching for her. I felt a nudge, but it wasn't her. It was the wolf. *This isn't working.*

You are not a quitter or a coward, child.

So now I was his child?

When you act like one, yes.

I hadn't meant for him to hear me whine. Frustration, fear, and shame boiled to the surface, and I fought like hell to keep the three counter-productive emotions in check. I fought for courage, searching my mind and my soul, for lack of a better word, to find what I hadn't even known I'd been missing. *Where are you, Coyote? I need you.*

I could feel the tickle of a presence, different from the wolf, but still not within my reach.

I need you. You are a part of me.

I squeezed my eyes shut and licked my dry lips, once again, exerting my thoughts to find her.

I blinked. I could move my eyes now. I'd licked my lips. The drug was wearing off. I threw all of my emotions behind my silent plea. *Come to me. Join with me.* Billy Bob had said I'd turned into a timber wolf. How long had it been since I'd shifted into coyote form? How long had I been without her and hadn't even noticed?

Since the full moon before my kidnapping. A year ago. Son-of-a-bitch. No wonder I had an empty place inside me. I'd created it. In accepting the wolf, I'd pushed aside my first form. *I'm sorry.* I told her. *I'm so sorry for leaving you behind.*

A soft whimper startled me. Me. I'd whimpered. Tears wet my cheeks. I could move my index fingers and my thumbs now. When my toes began to wiggle, I breathed deeply, fighting to keep a hold of both wolf and coyote. All the time I'd been captive, all the awful things those men did to me, I refused to transform. I refused to be part of their games. I'd buried my coyote, and she was having a hell of a time finding her way back. Brother Wolf said I needed them both.

I focused on the energy building around me. I accepted who I am. What I am. I'd wanted to live in the therian world. I'd wanted the community, but still, I'd resisted fully embracing my shifter side. Why did I hold back? Why was I so afraid to let go?

I could hear my mom's words, "We're not animals, Chav. We're human beings, forced to live like animals on the full moon." I thought she was wrong. I had never agreed with her about what we were. So, why did I only change when it was forced on me? I could be shifting every day, but other than when I'd been afraid two nights earlier, I'd only shifted on full moons when my beast could be in charge.

I concentrated on how good it had felt to transform into a wolf the second time that night, how the night air ruffled my fur, the scent of freshly blossomed wild roses, and Billy Bob. I remembered how safe he made me feel, even on four paws. My brain skipped forward to last night when he'd told me he loved me. When he proved it in so many ways how much he wanted me, and how I was the only one he wanted. Not Sunny. Not Bethany. Me.

My skin began to vibrate as I let his love fill me. As I embraced everything it meant to be his mate. I was wolf. I was coyote. I was woman. This would not be the end for me. This was not how I would exit this life.

The truck stopped suddenly, and I knew I had precious minutes before my captors came for me. I welcomed my beasts, allowing them to change me, allowing all three of us to become one.

The blood coursing through my arteries sounded as if I'd put a conch shell to my ear. Waves crashing on a shore. Through the noise, I heard a man say in a warped and hard to distinguish voice, "I have her. Don't call me an idiot. I was careful. No one saw me take her. Too many people watch her, so I took the opportunity. We only have one more day. The sacrifice has to happen before tomorrow's full moon. And we both know the third sacrifice has to be Chavvah Trimmel. We've known for almost a year she would be your salvation. Our deliverance. She was destined for us, and if this works, she will be our last. I'll call you when I have her prepared, until then, cover for me."

There were pauses during the conversation that I assumed was the other psycho responding, but even in animal form, the drug made the man sound as if he were talking underwater, and I couldn't hear the person he talked to at all. It felt weird being without my senses. One thing was certain, there were two of them. Maybe even more. Why did they think they needed me?

I focused on my breathing. I had to keep calm, stay sharp. Stay ready. When the tarp was pulled back, I leaped from my position on the bed, snarling and scratching out with my paws, as my kidnapper fell back, scrambling to get away. I didn't stick around to fight him. Even with my advantage, he could have a gun, and it was too dark after being pitched under a tarp for who-knew-how-long for my eyes to adjust quickly enough to catch a glimpse of him.

I could hear frantic shouting behind me as I took off deep into the woods. Gun shots rang out, making me glad I ran as quickly as I did. The man had smelled heavily of sassafras, and I promised myself I would force Babe to ban the substance from town if I got out of this alive.

The woods were dense with pines, elms, maples, and oak trees. Rocks, ditches, and underbrush didn't slow me down as I sprinted as fast as I could in the opposite direction of the killer. The moon was waxing gibbous, not quite full, but it would be tomorrow night. I was thankful I could still think for myself, even though on many levels, I wished my beasts could take over. In my race to get away, I realized I had no idea where I was.

I crossed three small streams, jumped over a few more ditches, some fallen timber, ignoring the smells of squirrels and raccoons (the real ones, not the therian variety), and I didn't stop until I found myself at the edge of a large lake. I didn't recognize the area. Densely forested woods and various bodies of water surrounded Peculiar. It had rolling hills and large flat areas. I certainly hadn't explored them all. Even so, I felt sure I was still in our community's land. The bridge had been shut down to the town. No one in. No one out.

I stopped and listened, sniffing the night air, drawing in a thousand scents around me, surprised at how easily I could distinguish each one. Having both wolf and coyote in me had its benefits. I didn't smell any humans. No predators. I waited. Other than a few brave tree frogs and crickets, I heard nothing else coming from the trees. Had I really escaped? Had I really managed to get away from the man who'd planned to make his *third sacrifice?*

Without meaning to, I transformed back to my human self. Naked, tired, but finally feeling safe, I let the relief wash over and around me.

You have done well, little wolf.

"Thanks," I said. "Where have you been?"

I was summoned.

"Billy Bob?"

Yes, the gray wolf called. He is worried for you. His mate.

I didn't like how pleased Brother Wolf sounded on that last bit. "Did you tell him I got away?"

Yes. He says to tell you he will tear heaven and earth apart to find you. He will not rest until you are safe and in his arms.

"Tell him that's kind of personal stuff to be relaying through a third party, but that I appreciate the sentiment." I know Brother Wolf saw me in his plane of existence, not in this one, but I wondered… "Tell the doc that I'm near a large lake, maybe the size of two football fields, the moon's reflection is to the right side. I didn't smell any human scents, so I don't think I'm near any homes."

Seconds passed.

I have done as you asked. He says to keep hidden and keep safe. He will find you.

I found a giant hollowed out tree nearby. I curled up in a ball, holding my knees tightly. As the adrenaline in my body waned, my lids and my limbs grew heavy with exhaustion, and I'm sure there was a little bit of the drug left in me as well. I didn't dare close my eyes. Didn't dare sleep. Billy Bob was coming for me. I just needed to stay vigilant and stay alive until he got here.

Strangely enough, I didn't cry. Unlike the last time I was kidnapped, this time, I'd gotten away. I might not be one-hundred percent safe, but I'd managed to save myself.

Not a victim, I told myself. Not this time.

I don't know how much time passed, but it had felt like three lifetimes when I heard the gentle pad of four paws on dried grass. I stayed hidden but leaned out from the tree enough to glimpse a large, gray wolf standing less than thirty feet away. His fur glowed as the moonlight turned it silvery-blue. His gaze captured mine, and I pushed myself to a stand, stumbling toward him. Jagged rocks dug into my bare feet, but I ignored the pain. The only important thing in my world was the wolf.

He bolted toward me, his body shifting on the way. By the time we met, closer to my side than the middle, Billy Bob grabbed me into his arms and clutched me so hard I couldn't breathe. His hands roamed my body as he examined me with his touch. Last, his fingers were in my hair, holding my head back so he could check my face.

"He didn't hit me," I told him. "He just knocked me out and hauled me out here in the back of his truck."

"Who?" Billy Bob asked in a way that promised violence, ending in a brutal death.

I shook my head. "I don't know. He drugged me with something. I couldn't move. I was paralyzed. He had a canvas tarp over me." I shook my head again. "I…I just can't tell you more."

"Can you describe him at all? His height? His weight? Hair color?"

"I was able to burn some of the drug from my body. Enough to shift." My voice cracked with emotion. "But everything seemed warped and weird, even for a while after I ran away."

He pulled me against his chest, the warmth of his skin easing the tension in my weary muscles. "It's okay," he murmured. "You're safe now. I have you, Chav, and I'm never letting you go."

My nose started to run. I sniffed. "But what if I have to pee?"

His tone was fierce. "Get used to an audience."

"I really do love you, Doc. But there is no way I can poop with you in the room."

A low growl rumbled gathered in his chest. "I will board up the bathroom window."

"Good, because watching me use the toilet might have been a deal breaker."

The low rumble turned into a chuckle. "You staked your claim on me at the Blonde Bear Café, Chav. There are no take backs."

I looked up at him pushed his silvery locks back from his face to drink in his raw, masculine beauty. He was everything. "No take backs," I agreed. "Will you take me home now?"

"My place." It wasn't a question. "We'll call the sheriff on the way. He can meet us there."

"My brain is still foggy," I said as I tried to remember more about the abduction.

"The tox screens came back on Wares and Blackwell. They'd both been dosed with a safrol, a drug extracted from the root of a sassafras tree used to make MDMA, and a paralytic compound. But the dose in both victims would have been enough to kill a human."

"Ecstasy?" It explained why I was super thirsty. I remember something more. "He knew about me."

"What?"

"The man who took me. I remember now. He said something about knowing last year that I would be the third sacrifice. That I was his or rather their destiny. He was talking on the phone with his partner. He said that I could be their deliverance."

"They can't have you. I won't let it happen. I can't lose you, Chavvah," he said. He kissed me gently. "Not when I've just found you."

"I'm not going anywhere," I told him. "I promise."

I hoped it was a promise I could keep.

CHAPTER 12

SHERIFF TAYLOR HAD COME out to take my statement personally. I wished I'd been able to tell him more, but a drugged up witness was almost as good as no witness at all. Apparently, I'd been gone for seven hours. Billy Bob and Sunny had reported me missing, and with the murder taking place at Sunny's Outlook two days earlier, the sheriff took my disappearance seriously. Billy Bob, in a frantic effort to find me, had gone full-on spirit ritual, body paint and all, in the hopes that Brother Wolf could reach out to me. I still didn't understand why the guardian spoke to me all the time, but I was glad I didn't have to work at finding him. Tonight could have ended much differently. Thank you, Brother Wolf.

You're welcome.

After a long, hot shower, I'd fallen asleep in Billy Bob's arms. When morning came, we were rudely awakened by the incessant push of the doorbell. The *ding-dong ding-dong* annoyed the hell out me.

Billy Bob pulled me into his arms, spooning me from behind, his peace pipe jabbing me in a sensitive place.

I giggled.

Don't judge me.

"There's someone at the door."

"They can wait," he said, nibbling my ear.

I groaned at the pleasure his love nips sent through my body. The doorbell kept ringing, but Billy Bob's hands on my breasts, his fingers teasing my nipples as his hot breath sizzled my skin pretty much meant I didn't care.

Finally, the noise stopped. I turned in his arms, my fingers slipping around his shaft. "You are frisky in the mornings."

He kissed the tip of my nose. "You bring out the pup in me, woman."

Oh lawd! The way he said woman tripped every hot, alpha fantasy I'd ever had. I moved closer until my breasts touched his chest, and leaned in for a heated, passionate kiss that scorched my brain with its fiery licks.

And just when my leg looped over his, giving him an all-access pass to my throbbing goodies, a loud banging on the window sent us flying apart and ready for battle.

A blonde I recognized all too well had her face pressed up against the window. She slapped the window pane again and then squinted. Her eyes grew large, much like Billy Bob's...you know. I yanked the cover up around me to hide my nakedness.

"Sunny!" I yelled.

She snapped her attention away from my naked boyfriend and stepped back from the window.

She managed a chagrinned, lopsided smile. "Open the door," she shouted, pointing sideways. She held up a white bag with her other hand. "I brought donuts."

I sighed with deep regret as I took in the Adonis in the room. I shrugged a half-apology. "She brought donuts."

"I can't compete with donuts." He turned his back to me and grabbed a pair of jeans off the back of a chair.

I cussed Sunny ten ways to Sunday for her ill-timed interruption as he pulled them up over his sexy ass. I didn't know when or how, but my ex-BFF was going pay. I got dressed too, mourning the loss of morning nookie.

Billy Bob started the coffee while I answered the door. Sunny had a fake as hell smile plastered on her face as she held out the bag. I gave her a dirty look and gestured for her to come in.

I closed the door and relocked it. Leftover nerves from the night before. When I turned around to follow Sunny to the kitchen, she pitched herself into my arms. The wet of her tears smeared on my cheek.

"Oh, Chav," she said, squeezing me with more strength than an anaconda. "Why are you always getting kidnapped?"

"I don't know." I put my arms around her to complete the hug. "I must have 'take me' tattooed on my forehead."

She leaned back, grabbed my chin, and tilted my head down. She examined my face very carefully. "Nope," she said. "No tattoos. Just a few wrinkles and some ghastly clogged pores."

I gasped in horror. "Sunshine Ambrosia Haddock. You are an awful human being."

She sniffed and nodded. "Yes," she said. She wiped at her eyes and managed a genuine smile. "I really am."

We both began to laugh, and the tension I hadn't even realized I'd been holding inside released like a cake in a well-greased pan.

"Coffee's ready," Billy Bob said.

Sunny and I turned to see him standing in the archway leading back to the kitchen. He wore a black T-shirt that fit snug across his wide chest, and damn, he made those tight jeans look mmm-mmm-good.

Sunny gave me side-eye, her eyebrow raised.

I gave her side-eye back and wiggled my brows.

Billy Bob shook his head, chuckling softly, as he went back into the kitchen giving us both a very nice view of him walking away.

"Holy shit, Chav," Sunny said in a quiet voice. "You and Billy Bob. I am seriously impressed."

"What? You didn't think I could land a man like the doc?"

She wrapped her arm around my waist and put her head on my shoulder. "Don't be silly. I'm impressed he managed to land you. You are a fucking catch, and any man would be goddamn lucky to have you in his life."

I don't know why, but I teared up. Not enough that anything leaked from my eyes, but I think on some level, I was almost afraid I was too damaged for any relationship. I rubbed her shoulder. "Thanks, Sunny. You always know the right thing to say."

"Yeah," she said. "It's a gift."

We laughed again. "That coffee smells good."

"Well, let's go get some then." She picked her donut bag off the floor.

"Cinnamon twist?"

"You bet." She winked. "A cinnamon twist for you, old fashions for Billy Bob, and a double chocolate dipped raspberry éclair with extra raspberry for me."

"So you really are pregnant."

She grinned. "I'll wait until after the Jubilee and we find these fucking bastards before I take the official test." She glanced at Billy Bob, who had already poured three cups of coffee and set the steaming mugs on the counter.

"Have you told Babe?"

"Do you think I would have said it in front of Billy Bob if I hadn't?"

"I guess not." I chuckled, so glad I had her in my life. She was right. Babe would have had a conniption if she had told Billy Bob about her pregnancy before him.

"Congratulations, Sunny." He pushed her mug to her. "You can come in anytime during clinic hours. I'll work you in."

"Of course, you will," I said, more out of habit than a real belief that he preferred Sunny to me. He'd pretty much kissed and…well…you know… the doubt right out of me.

Sunny smacked me. "So, tell me what happened, and don't you dare leave a single thing out. I may get an impression or something."

"We should be safe for tonight. The killer has to be a therian, so he'll be shifting along with the rest of us."

"They grabbed you in broad daylight," Sunny said. "If they want to kill someone today, they will find a way to do it, and I want to help stop them."

"You're right," I said. "The man the night before had seemed determined to get in a third killing before the full moon."

"Sunny," Billy Bob said. "Trying to get a vision while you're pregnant isn't a good idea."

She narrowed her gaze on him. "My baby is the size of a cashew. She doesn't even have a nervous system yet, let alone a brain. She will not be traumatized by any visions I get, but I will certainly be traumatized if we don't catch these psychos before they kill someone I love."

He didn't look completely convinced, but, finally, he nodded. Good thing too, because I'd known Sunny for almost a decade, and she wasn't going to let him stop her from doing what she wanted to do.

Sunny took my hand and closed her eyes.

"We're doing this now?"

She peeked at me with one eye. "Now is as good a time as any."

"Fine." I sighed. "What do you want me to do?"

"Focus on yesterday. Everything you can remember. Try to picture it in your mind as you do."

"Okay." I put my thoughts to the day before.

"After the public make-out," Sunny said.

I blushed hotly. I hadn't meant to go back that far, but wow, it was hard to forget climbing up my man in a public eatery. "You saw that?"

"Along with half the town."

Oh yeah. I'd forgot about the recording.

Sunny kept her eyes shut. "And while it was very exciting, it's not going to help us find the bad guys."

"Does this mean your gift is working?"

"It's like I'm watching TV with an old UHF antenna, everything is grainy, and I'm only getting a partial picture, but yes, I see bits and pieces."

"Gotcha." I tried to only sift through the memories after entering Sunny's Outlook. The sharp prick in my neck. Waking up in the back of a truck. The rough roads leading into the woods. Brother Wolf.

Do you need something, little sister?

Oops. I hadn't meant to call him. He had been a major part of how I'd managed to escape.

A strange look passed over Sunny's face. "Who is Brother Wolf?" she asked. "Does Billy Bob have a brother?"

"No," I heard the doc say. "He is Chavvah's spirit guardian."

"Huh. I'll expect a full explanation later," she said. "But keep thinking about the Brother Wolf dude. I am getting a stronger signal when he's in the picture."

I couldn't help but think about when I first started hearing his voice while kept in a cage. Brother Wolf had been a way to escape the metal bars. He'd help me escape the pain.

"Oh, honey," Sunny said. "It was so awful for you."

"What do you see?" Billy Bob asked.

"The cage she was kept in at the lodge." She held up a hand to silence Billy Bob's next question. "I can see a shadowy figure in a stretch of green pastures and blue streams. The sky is the color of sapphires, and the clouds are ridiculously fluffy and white as if giant cotton balls levitated in the air.

"He is a giant wolf. Black as night with eyes that are the color of white diamonds." She took a deep breath and held it for a moment. "I can hear him talk to you, Chavvah. I hear him tell you that you are not alone. That you are his child."

I wanted to cry as she spoke. I remembered that day so clearly. The hunters had broken my collarbone trying to make me turn. I almost did. Brother Wolf, even when I didn't have a name to call him, had lent me his strength.

"Where is this place?" Sunny asked with wonder.

It is the aether, Brother Wolf said. *It is the place where I exist.*

"It's the spirit world," I told her. "It's where my guardian lives."

I can show you, sister. I can show you through the seer.

Yes. Without hesitation. *Yes.*

In the next second, I was standing in a field with Brother Wolf. I was in animal form as well now, and judging by the size of my paws, I'd appeared as the timber wolf, not the coyote. I gave my first nature a gentle apology.

I saw then what Brother Wolf saw. A curled up woman, damaged but not broken, on the ground in front of him. He could see me in the cage, but he couldn't see the cage. He could see the result of the physical abuse on my body, but not the attackers. I understood now why he couldn't have guided Billy Bob to my location. We were in a realm where time and place didn't matter.

"Is this the past?"

"There is no past, present, or future here. Time is irrelevant."

"So that…" I pointed to my battered visage. "…is happening to me now?"

"Yes," he said sadly, his voice no longer in my head. The large black wolf shook his head. "You are strong, child. You are brave."

I looked at the helpless version of myself. "I don't feel it."

"Fear is not weakness. Fear keeps you alive. Weakness is a failure to act because of fear. This is not the case with you."

Enduring my torture had been wretched, but I imagined it must have been awful to watch.

"It is." Brother Wolf rubbed his muzzle against mine.

I forgot this wasn't a memory for him. Just as I was beside him in the *aether*, I was also, for him, still in the cage.

Across the meadow, movement caught my eye. A coyote ran across the field, his body blurring and blinking as if it struggled to keep form.

"Who is that?" I asked

"A visitor."

"To what purpose?"

"His own, I suppose. He has come in his upright form many times, but lately, he transforms into coyote when he approaches."

I was curious how many of us could communicate with the guardians. "Is he like me? A spirit talker?"

"He has made himself one."

"What do you mean?"

"He is not mine. I know nothing more."

The scenery around me began to blink, to fade. The girl I'd been only a year ago disappeared. I wanted to reach out to her, to comfort her, to tell her that help was coming. She knew it was on the way.

I mean, I knew it.

I didn't have to go back to be saved. A flickering of images staggered me. Fur, blood, exposed muscle. A curved blade used with surgical precision. The strong scent of sassafras. Someone chanted. I tried to raise my hands to my ears, but I couldn't move. Was I paralyzed? Had they found me again? Had I been taken?

The star. The eight-point star. Not made of twigs. Not mine.

It covered the naked back of the killer. He stopped mid-slice. And pivoted slowly to stare at the place where I watched. Only, he didn't have a face. Not a human one. Oh my God. If this was a dream, I wanted to wake up.

"Chavvah!" The rough shaking of my shoulders roused me. "Chavvah!" It was Billy Bob. He and Sunny were crouched over me, and I was on the floor blinking up at them.

I screamed as I sat up. I tried with all my might to stop picturing what I had just seen. It could have been me. "Oh, God." I shook my head when Billy Bob tried to help me up. "His face. It was a black bear face, but it wasn't his. Christ. He wore Mike like a second skin."

"I know," Sunny said.

I looked at her then and saw my own horror reflected in her eyes. I'd always thought it would be cool to have her psychic ability, but now… "How do you live with that, Sunny? How?"

My hair stuck to my sweaty cheeks, and Sunny brushed it away from my eyes with her fingers. "I get up in the morning, brush my teeth, wash my face, and maybe have breakfast." I appreciated her efforts toward humor, but her bleak smile said how she really felt. "It's not bad all the time. You know that, Chav."

Billy Bob lifted me then. "No more of that," he said.

"Agreed." I was in no hurry to see visions or visit the spirit world again.

"Tell him about the star," Sunny said.

"The killer had an eight-point star tattooed on his back. I didn't see if he had any other marks." I rubbed my upper arms as if to ward off a chill. "I think we should start with Hans Fisk. I saw the edge of a tattoo on his upper arm."

"Lots of people have tattoos," Billy Bob said. "We need a better reason to examine the man."

"Yes, but this one was a star." I crossed my arms.

"Okay." Billy Bob mimicked my stance, and the way it made his pecs dance when he crossed his arms, made my nipples rigid. He flicked a glance at them, a half smile tugging at his lips. "We'll go talk to Sheriff Taylor."

"Great," Sunny said. "Chavvah can ride with me." She tugged at my arm. "We have much to discuss."

Billy Bob stopped her by pulling me back. "You are going to your cabin, Sunny, and locking the door. The full moon is tonight, and as the day gets closer to sundown, everyone is going to be feeling antsy. You need to lock yourself in and stay safe."

"He's right," I said.

Sunny green eyes widened with betrayal. "Et tu, Chav?"

"Just go home, Sunny. You've helped so much. We know more now because of you, but today is going to be hard enough if I'm worried about you as well as these killers."

"More than one?"

"Yes. Even though we only saw one in your vision. The guy who took me was talking to a partner on the phone. Please go home. You and baby Jude need to keep safe until this is all over."

To my relief, she nodded. "I'll go. But call me today if you find out anything new. Or call me if you don't. I'm going to go crazy out at that cabin by myself, knowing all this stuff is happening, and I can't do a damn thing about it."

I gave her a quick, brief hug. "You got it, sweetie. You're the best."

"Again," she said, in her very Sunny way. "I know."

CHAPTER 13

THE SHERIFF'S DEPARTMENT bustled as the cataloging of citizens and visitors continued. They hadn't made much headway on my kidnapping, but since I'd been there and had no idea who had taken me, I guess I couldn't really blame them. What I could blame them for was the immediate cessation of talking and the obvious gawking as Billy Bob and I walked in.

I crossed my arms and glared at every person with the nerve to meet my eyes. I almost shrugged Billy Bob's hand off the middle of my back as he guided me to Sheriff Taylor's office, but really, that small display of affection was nothing compared to me climbing him like a greased pole at the fair.

Sheriff Taylor beckoned us into his office. He closed the door behind Billy Bob and me. "Take a seat." His shoulders slumped, and his voice sounded weary. He shook his head as if to clear the cobwebs, then met my gaze. "Dr. Smith says you have more information. Did you remember something new?"

"Not exactly." I wasn't sure how much to tell. He'd barely believed Sunny last year about her psychic ability. Telling him I was talking to spirits might not make me the most credible witness. I decided to go with a half-truth. "Sunny came over to Billy Bob's this morning around six."

Sheriff Taylor raised a questioning brow. "She's planning on staying in tonight, right?"

"Yes. She's not dumb." Which is not to say that she always makes good choices, because, I'm pretty sure everyone knows that's not true. "She had a vision."

"Yeah? I thought her radar was on the fritz."

"Apparently, it got a jump start this morning." I let my exasperation shine on my face. "This would go a lot faster if you'd just let me get through it."

He rolled his hand at me as if to say, "It's your show."

"She saw a man with a curved skinning blade." I gagged as I thought of him. "He had an eight-point star tattooed on his back." For a moment, I was afraid to even blink. Afraid that I'd be back in that room again with the monster. "She couldn't see his face. He was wearing his victim's half-form face. It was a black bear."

"Does she think it could have been Mike? Or a new victim?"

I frowned. I hadn't even thought about a future prediction. I'd just assumed it was a past killing. How could I be so presumptuous? "Honestly, I don't know." My phone rang. It was Sunny. "Hold on, I better take this." I tapped my phone. "Hey, everything okay?"

"Have you seen Jo Jo?" she asked.

I tucked my chin. "No. I called him after you left to tell him we wouldn't be opening today. But I haven't seen him. Why?"

"Brady called. He said he's been trying Jo Jo's phone and can't get an answer. He was hoping we were keeping him busy." I could hear the worry in her tone.

"I'm sure he's fine, Sunny. He's young and full of…well, youth. He's probably on some secret rendezvous with Michele Thompson."

"I hope so. Call me if you hear anything."

"You got the doors locked?"

"Yes, mother."

"Good. I'll call you later." I hung up.

"Jo Jo's missing?" Billy Bob asked.

"Not sure. His dad can't get ahold of him by phone. It could be a case of dead battery." I prayed like hell it wasn't a case of dead kid.

Sheriff Taylor leaned forward. "You think he might be with Michele? Maybe you should call Ruth and see if the girl is home or not."

The sheriff's worry increased my anxiety. I called Ruth. "Hey," I said when she answered. "Is Michele at home?"

"She went out early today, Chav. What's up?"

I didn't want to alarm Ruth, especially if this turned out to be a lovers' tryst. "I thought she might be interested in a job. We have the whole Tri-Council to feed tomorrow, and I can use the extra help."

"I'll let her know." I could feel Ruth's pride through the phone, and it made me sick with guilt.

"Can you give me her phone number? I'll call her myself."

"Sure! And then maybe later you can tell me all about you and certain leggy werewolf doctor."

My cheeks flared with heat. I knew both Billy Bob and Sheriff Taylor could hear her. "Uhm, sure."

I got Michele's number and hung up with Ruth. My call went straight to voicemail. "I could be nothing," I said, trying to convince myself.

Billy Bob stood up behind me and kneaded my shoulders. "We should look for them."

"Agreed," Sheriff Taylor said. "We shouldn't take any chances."

I reached up and clutched Billy Bob's hand on my shoulder. "What if they have him? They said they needed a third sacrifice before the full moon, and since I escaped…" Was this my fault? Had they taken Jo Jo because they couldn't have me?

Deputy Farrady knocked on the sheriff's door then poked his head in the room. "Brady Corman is here. He says he found Jo Jo's car abandoned on the side of the road between their house and town."

Out in the main room, Brady looked almost wild with panic.

"Is he drinking again?" I heard Tyler Thompson ask.

Brady turned on him, his amber eyes dilated with fear. "No, I'm not fucking drinking, you jackass. My son has been taken."

"Now, Brady," the sheriff said. "We don't know that for sure. Calm down, and we'll get to the bottom of this. We were just getting ready to go look for him."

Brady's dark brown hair pitched into his face as he opened his hand and stared down at his palm. He held a set of car keys and an eight-point star, this one made of metal. His voice was hollow as he spoke. "I found his truck pulled off to the side of the road. The driver's side door was open, the keys were still in the ignition, his phone was plugged into his charger, and this star was in the middle of his seat." He slapped the keys and the star onto Farraday's desk. "Someone's taken my boy."

His eyes were sunken and weary as he spun around. Willy Boden held out a Styrofoam cup. "Here," she said, holding the steaming cup out to him. "Would you like some coffee?"

"I'd really like a shot of whiskey," Brady said. "But that won't bring my son home."

She set the cup down and nodded. "Okay."

I knew she was trying to be kind, and I'm glad she hadn't gotten mad when he didn't respond well to her gesture. Brady had already lost his wife to the same hunters who'd kidnapped me the year before, and he'd barely survived her loss. If something happened to Jo Jo, it would kill him.

"Ms. Boden has offered her assistance in this matter. She has contacts with the FBI," Sheriff Taylor said.

That explained her presence. I wondered how much she knew about what was going on in our town. She was security for the Tri-Council. If her brother was the killer, she could be helping him hide his tracks.

Brady blinked then looked at me. "We have to find my kid."

It was ten in the morning now. Dusk would hit around eight-thirty. Impulsively, I casually put my hand over the metal star, took it up, and placed it into my pocket. It was as if I needed to possess the damn thing, the same way I had with the wooden one. Holding the new one made me realize how much I'd lost when I'd left the other behind in the killer's truck.

I put my hand on Brady's shoulder. "We only have ten hours before the full moon, so we better organize search parties. We can start in Tiller Woods, but really, we should search anywhere there's a lot of unsettled acres." Men needed to "do" things when they were worried. It made them feel like they had some control in an uncontrollable situation.

Brady nodded fiercely, ready to go. However, Deputy Farraday, Connelly, and Thompson all stared at the sheriff, waiting for his orders.

He snapped his fingers. "You heard Miss Trimmel. Do you have to be told twice? Call the town together, and let's get search parties going."

Brady slumped against the desk, bumping the coffee. It spilled. "Shit," he said jumping up.

"I got it," Willy said. She grabbed a box of tissue from Farraday's desk and started pulling out wads of it to soak of the spill.

The heavy scent of the black coffee permeated the air. Brady looked up at me. "I can't do this again."

I took his hand. "You won't have to. We're going to find him, Brady. We're going to find him and bring him home."

Deputy Connelly carried over his tablet. On the screen was a topographical map of Peculiar and the surrounding area. He held it out for Brady. "Where did you find his truck?"

My phone rang again. It was Ruth. I picked up the call.

"I can't find Michele."

Those four words chilled me to the bone. "Where did she say she was going?"

"She didn't," Ruth said. "She's nineteen-years-old, Chav. She doesn't always tell me where she's off to."

My stomach sank. "I think you better come over to the police station."

"Why?"

Damn it. I didn't know what to say. There was no logical reason for the killers to take two people. The murders had been organized, ritualistic. Two victims wouldn't follow the pattern. "Jo Jo Corman's been taken. We could use your help."

I heard her gasp. "You don't think…"

"I really don't, but just in case, you should be here."

"I'm on my way." She hung up without another word.

Twenty minutes later, most of the town and many of the Jubilee attendees crowded the courthouse lawn. They were divided up into groups and given sections of land to scour. Ruth and Ed had both come, along with their son Taylor, Tyler's twin, and their next oldest Dakota, to join the search. They stood near Brady—all of them huddled for comfort in a way that made my heart break.

Dominic approached our group, which made Billy Bob squeeze my fingers until I thought my nails would pop off. "Ease up, Doc."

"I don't like him."

"I get that, but he's really a nice guy." Absently, I put my hand in my pocket to touch the star I'd lifted from the deputy's desk.

"Uh huh," he said, looking wholly unconvinced.

"Chavvah." Dominic flashed me a smile then frowned at Billy Bob. "Dr. Smith."

"Tartan," Billy Bob said.

"Ow." I pinched the top of his hand with my free one until he eased up on his hold. "Do you know where Hans Fisk is? Is he off with the Lowry brothers?"

Dominic's cheeks dented as if he were chewing on the inside. Finally, he said, "I saw Hans and Bethany Hilliard earlier."

"Together?"

He shrugged. "It was probably politics. It got pretty heated."

Could Bethany and Hans be in on the killings together? After all, he'd left the restaurant before me yesterday. He would have had time to get into the restaurant ahead of me. "Hmmm. How early?"

Jo Jo had been gone before Brady had gotten up, and he'd called Sunny around eight.

"I'm not sure. A couple of hours ago maybe."

"And you," I asked. "Where were you this morning?"

"Am I a suspect, Chavvah?"

I hadn't seriously considered Dom a suspect, but his reluctance to answer the question made me suspicious.

Billy Bob had been quiet up until then. "Everyone we don't know is a suspect, Tartan. You could be one of the killers as easy as anyone."

"Now, Doc. He was still at the restaurant when I got nabbed yesterday."

He turned his dark gaze on me with swift rebuke. "There are two of them, Chav. You don't think one of them could have been out in the public while the other did the dirty work."

Ouch. I hated to admit it, but my knight in shining gray fur had a point. Only, I wasn't going to let anyone treat me like a damsel in distress.

"Is Sunny going to join the search?" Dominic asked just as casually as I had posed my question.

My hackles rose. "What do you want with Sunny?"

"I just…" He shook his head, and his shoulders slumped. "I heard she had…gifts." He almost rolled his eyes then as if the word psychic was too dirty for his mouth.

Well, fuu-uck you, Dominic Tartan. "She has a gift for having babies. That's about all, as far as I know."

He crossed his arms. "I thought we were friends, Chavvah."

I put my hand out to stop Billy Bob from advancing on Dom. Sheesh. I'd never seen the man this tense before. It was a sharp departure from the usually laid-back country doctor. "There are friends," I said to Dom. "Then there are friends."

"You can trust me," he said softly.

"Enough," Billy Bob said. "Go find another group, Tartan. This one is full up."

I shook my hand free of the dominant werewolf's and glared at him. He didn't back down with the eye contact, which almost made me look away. Almost. "You don't own me, Billy Bob Smith, and I'll be damned if I'm going to let you treat me like a possession. You can trust me to not jump the bones of every man who looks my way, or we can end it here and now because I won't have it."

He looked away then. That's right. This girl was not a pushover.

Babe came over to us then. He raised a brow at the sulky doctor. "Doc Smith." He nodded to me. "Chavvah."

I leaned over and kissed his cheek. "Hey, bro. We need to get this show on the road. Time's a tickin,' and if anything happens to Jo Jo or Michele..." My chest squeezed tight as I allowed myself to envision the worse. "...I don't know how I'd..."

Billy Bob put his arm around me for comfort, and as a way of forgiving him his he-man routine, I allowed it.

"We'll find him, Chavvah," Babe said.

Sheriff Taylor sent everyone off to do their grid search, but when he got to our group, he took Babe, Billy Bob, and me aside. Quietly, he said, "We've gotten new information from the FBI. I did a search for similar killings in Kansas, Arkansas, Oklahoma, Tennessee, and Illinois. I found hits and misses going back as long as they have been keeping records, but five years ago there was a missing person's filed on a man in Kansas. They found his body out by a ditch on I-70 between Topeka and Wichita. He'd been skinned, his throat slit. I looked the man up. His name was David Brooks, and he was a registered therian, half-vulpes, half-lycan from Midland Grove, one of the Kansas communities."

Billy Bob and I exchanged looks. Was it a coincidence the victims were hybrid-therians or was that the commonality, the reason they were chosen?

Sheriff Taylor continued, "No other murders were reported, but I suspect, someone started covering up the killings. If it hadn't been for a human finding David Brooks, I think his death would have stayed a secret as well."

He didn't have to say "like the deaths we covered up in Peculiar last year." It was a given. We tried to keep our tragedies and the way we dealt with injustices in-house.

"If this goes back five years, or at least that we know of, these guys have had a lot of time to perfect their tradecraft."

The sheriff nodded solemnly. "I'm afraid so."

"We need to get out there now, Sheriff. We have to find Jo Jo." I could feel the panic welling again inside.

You cannot help him if you are not clear of mind, sister.

I can't help him at all! I felt useless. Worse than useless. Helpless.

"What is it?" Billy Bob asked.

"Just my invisible cheerleader trying to give me a pep talk."

"Brother Wolf?" He sounded surprised.

"Yeah. Him." I felt as grumpy as I sounded. "What good is it having a spirit guardian when he can't even see anything on this plane of existence but me? I need him to see Jo Jo, to tell me where he is!"

"You and I are going to have a long talk when this is over."

I detected a hint of awe and jealousy. Surely, he didn't think Brother Wolf would put the moves on me.

The gray one is a complicated beast. He wonders why you can talk to me to easily when he must use rituals.

I didn't have time for a pissing contest over spiritual matters.

I got my brother's attention. "Billy Bob and I are going. I have a good sniffer, and his is awesome. I'll call if we find him."

Babe nodded. "I'll do the same."

I looked at my watch. It was just past eleven a.m. I felt chilled to the bone as I thought about how quickly they could skin Jo Jo alive. I'd seen one of the killers work with deft efficiency, and I could only hope they would wait. "We have to find him." I rubbed my arms. "We have to."

* * * *

The aroma of pine, peat moss, dirt, and lake water barely made a dent against the stench of my fear. I hadn't thought I would have such a visceral reaction to being back in these woods. Obviously, I'd thought wrong. The temperature was nearing the high nineties, and the humidity had sweat rolling down the crack of my ass.

"We should change. It will increase our ability to find Jo Jo," Billy Bob said.

I knew he was right. Most of our group, Ruth and Ed, their boys Tyler and Taylor, Brady Corman, Willy Boden, Chance Lowry, Kyle Avery, and several others had already dropped their clothes and shifted. I was surprised to see Chance had shifted into coyote form. His father Jacob was a beaver. I wondered if he knew what kind of danger being hybrid put him in. Though, why had they taken me? I was pretty sure no one knew that I'd been able to turn into a wolf. Maybe my theory about hybrid-breeds being the target for these killers was wrong.

Whatever their motivation, I wasn't sure I could bring my coyote to the surface, not as easily as the wolf, and I wasn't ready for people aka Babe to know yet that I had another animal form. *I'm so petty*, I thought. While it wasn't a certainty, I knew in my heart Jo Jo was in extreme danger. I needed to get over myself.

"Okay," I said, my heart thumping in my throat. I rubbed my clammy, wet palms together and braced my courage. I could do this. Finding Jo Jo was the only thing that mattered. I took my clothes off and passed them to Billy Bob. He took his clothes off, and his woody was looking log-ish.

"I can't help it," he muttered, staring uncomfortably straight ahead. "It happens every time I'm around you."

"Flatteringly inappropriate," I said.

"Tell me about it." He shook his head, his silver hair sticking like rivulets of ore to his heat-damp shoulders. Within seconds, the fur on his body sprouted then laid down as his body morphed into a large gray wolf. I sighed. He made it look so easy.

God, it should be easy. It was a part of me. A part of me I'd wanted to embrace. Otherwise, why even move to Peculiar? I thought about my coyote. I imagined her looking much like Babel and Judah. Reddish-brown fur, thinner, less blocky nose than the wolf, a bushy brown tail with a variety of red, white, and black hair mixed in. I felt myself changing, shifting down. In this form, I could feel the pull of the thunder moon. Its lunar energy called to my beast. Unable to stop myself, I leaned my head back and howled.

Billy Bob's gray wolf joined in. Soon, howls and other creature noises joined in with mine as we all skirted the eighty acres with one thought in mind. *Find Jo Jo.*

Five hours of searching yielded nothing. Billy Bob and I trotted back to his truck. Both of us shifting, him getting wood again, and me giving him the eye. We quickly dressed to avoid any further conversation. I checked my phone. I had three text messages from Sunny.

First text message said: **Just checking in. Keep me informed.**

The second message said: **Do you know someone with a white pick-up truck?**

My stomach squeezed.

The third message said: **I have ur friend. Find a way to come to her cabin alone or her blood will be on ur hands.**

Oh my God, oh my God. I wanted to scream my horror. *Keep it together, Chav. You can't let Sunny down. You can't.*

You should tell the gray one.

"Shut up," I said through gritted teeth.

"What?" Billy Bob asked. "I didn't say anything. Any news?" He glanced at the phone clutched in my hands.

"No," I said, trying hard to keep my voice normal. I knew he'd be able to hear my racing heart and my quicker breaths, so I really focused on slowing it all down. *Her blood will be on your hands.* No. I wouldn't fail Sunny.

"Sunny is out of diapers, and she needs them for Jude. Is it okay if I take your truck?" I swallowed at the lie. "I'll bring it back as soon as possible."

"I'll go with you," he said.

"No." I shook my head. "Jo Jo needs everyone searching for him, and you're his best bet, Doc." I pointed to my nose. "You've got the most developed sense of smell. I'd never forgive myself if we didn't get to him in time. Please stay."

He furrowed his brow at me, holding his stare on my face until he finally gave me a quick nod. He handed me the keys. "Hurry back."

As a desperate act of a dying woman, I threw myself into his arms, and I kissed him with every bit of passion, anger, grief, and love I could muster. If this would be the last time I could touch him, I wanted to remember every second of how he tasted on my lips. When we stopped kissing after several long seconds, Billy Bob said, "What was that about?'

"I'm just going to miss you, is all." I gave him a quick peck and jingled the keys. "I'll be back as soon as I can."

"Promise?"

"Cross my heart," I told him.

"I love you, Chavvah."

"I know," I said, the emotion choking my words. I couldn't say it back. I was betraying him by leaving and putting myself into the hands of a killer, and I hated myself for it. But this was Sunny… Eventually, I hoped, he would forgive me.

CHAPTER 14

ALL THE WAY TO SUNNY'S, my mind raced with scenarios. Who was this killer? Why had he picked Sunny? She wasn't even a therianthrope. Fuck. A tourist wouldn't know that about her. We'd been passing her off as a shifter since the Jubilee had started. Would he be torturing her now to try and get her to shift? And what about baby Jude? Fuck. I'd been so caught up in my worry for Sunny that I'd forgotten my nephew in the process.

Her driveway was just ahead. What if I couldn't save her on my own? What if the killers decided on a two for one special and just murdered both of us? I'd been scared when I got the text, and I'd acted rashly. I drove past her drive without stopping. I parked about half a mile up and around a sharp curve. Taking deep breaths, I prayed for some guidance.

You should tell your mate.

That's not helpful, I told Brother Wolf. *If you want to be a real help, go see if Sunny and Jude are okay.*

I cannot see your friend. She is not of my blood.

Awesome. I might as well have had Casper the Ghost at my side.

You are strong, little wolf, but you are stronger with your mate.

My phone beeped with another text. This time, there was a picture attached. Sunny was tied to a chair in her kitchen, her right eye was swollen, and her lip was smeared with blood.

1 sacrifice is as good as another, the message said. **U better hurry if U want to save ur friend.**

I looked at Sunny's picture again, the rage curling inside me, filling me until it spilled over my skin. There was no time to plan. Sunny and Jude needed me now. I ran through the woods, stretching my legs in long strides, amazed at my agility. I sent a silent thank you to Brother Wolf. He might not like me trying to rescue my friend alone, but he hadn't deserted me. I'd never moved this fast in human form. It took me seconds, not minutes, to get to the backside of the cabin. I stalked quietly around the perimeter of the house, careful to keep low. In the photograph, Sunny had been tied up in the kitchen. Would she still be there? I snuck a look through the side window. Sunny's African violets she kept on the ledge over the sink helped hide me from view. Her backside was to me, and her head slumped.

My pulse skittered. Was she dead? Her hands were tied behind her back. I saw her fingers flex. Dead people didn't flex. Relief staggered me. A large being, reminding me so much of Brother Wolf's shadow man form, walked into the room. I suppressed the urge to retch. He wore the skins of his previous victims, even over his face. I could imagine Sunny's fears. It should have been me in his grasp, not her. I could survive more physical trauma than her, take more abuse. Sunny was human. Frail.

He doesn't know that, I thought. *He thinks she's one of us.*

Oh, Sunny. In our efforts to protect her, we'd turned her into a target. No, I thought. Being my best friend had made her a target. I could go around to the back door off the kitchen and burst through. *The element of surprise might be all I need,* I thought, trying to delude myself into action.

The fur-wearing lunatic bent over, and I watched as he retrieved something from behind him. My stomach lurched and my brain went numb at the sight in his arms. Jude. In his arms, my sweet nephew reached out for his mom.

Sunny screamed, "I'll kill you!" as she struggled to break the bindings around her wrists.

"You have a sweet child, Mrs. Trimmel." He stroked a finger down the side of Jude's face. "I'd hate for anything to happen to him because your friend decides to play hero." He turned to the window where

I watched. "Are you planning on being a hero, Chavvah?"

My gut twisted. He knew I was there. This man, no, this monster had me by the short hairs. Even if Jude hadn't been involved, I would have gladly traded myself for Sunny, but now with the baby in the mix, it was the only option.

My phone vibrated in my pocket. *Not now.* I pulled it out. Incoming from Billy Bob. I hit the ignore button. He called again. Damn it. I couldn't think. I just needed a minute to think.

A message beeped on my phone: **Found Jo Jo and Michele. Tied up in the woods, but safe. Where are you?**

Thank God they're safe, was my first thought. My second thought was, had their kidnapping been a distraction so the killers could grab Sunny while everyone was focused on Jo Jo? How could I have been so naïve? The bad guys had been a step ahead of me and everyone else at every turn. This mad man held my precious nephew in his arms, he'd accosted my best friend, tied her up and battered her, and I had done exactly what he wanted. I delivered myself like an early Christmas present.

Where are you? Another text from Billy Bob.

So much anger and raged welled inside me. I finally knew what it was to be loved. Would he mourn me like Brady had mourned Rose Ann? I should have told him. I should have trusted him.

"Come out, come out, Chavvah. Time is ticking," the monster taunted.

I glanced down at my phone again, quickly I swiped in: **He has Sunny and Jude. Going in. Forgive me. I love you.**

I set the phone on the ground, cringing as it blew up with text after text as I walked around the side of the house. "If you want me, you can have me, but only if you let Sunny and the baby go first." I had no real room for negotiation, but I had to try.

"I can kill her now," the man said. "If that's what you want."

I gripped the door handle. "Don't," I said loud enough for him to hear me. "I'm coming in."

He laughed. The cadence sounded familiar to me as if I heard that laugh before, but the mask distorted the sound.

"Oh, Chav," Sunny said when I walked into the house.

"I'm here, hon. Just hang in there." The left side of her face was a bright shade of candy red and blood dripped from the corner of her mouth.

I snarled and lunged forward, but the creep held up Jude between us, effectively stopping me in my tracks. This close to him, I could smell the rot of death all over him, and under that, sassafras.

"Why?" I asked. "What is with the sassafras?"

He cradled Jude back in his arms, a muffled coo as he rubbed the five-month-old's belly. "My mother used to bath me using a mixture of lavender and sassafras oil. She believed it to be a gift from the gods. A way to create a direct conduit to the spirits. She wasn't wrong."

"Please put my baby down," Sunny said. "He's innocent."

"Aren't we all?" The killer looked up at me. His eyes were like black marbles in the shade of the bear mask. "I'm so close, Chavvah. You have no idea how long I've waited. When I saw you in that cage—"

"Wait. What? How did you see me?" God, maybe he had been one of the guards. Impossible, I thought, but my old fears crept in.

"The same way I saw you two nights ago. You are like me. You can cross into the between. I saw you staring at yourself in that cage. The same way I saw you a year ago. It's the reason I'm here. The reason we're all here." He sounded jubilant and self-assured. This maniac was drinking his own Kool-Aid. Even so, I believed him about the spirit realm.

"Are you the coyote that I saw running across the field?" I moved closer, putting myself between him and Sunny.

I couldn't see his smile, but I could hear it in his voice. "Yes. I'm so glad you saw me. That form is magnificent. I'm only truly free when I'm there." He leaned close, holding Jude tighter and whispered, "I want to be free here."

"You're nuts if you think you're going to get away with this."

"Don't poke the crazy," Sunny muttered.

He pulled handcuffs from under the furs he wore and threw them at me. I caught them. They looked like standard police issue, but what the hell did I know?

"Cuff yourself to the fridge handle."

Reluctantly I did as he asked. The metal bit into my wrists. "Now, put Jude down."

"I'm a man of my word, Chavvah." He bent over and put Jude back into the baby carrier. He set Jude down by Sunny, and I could see some of the tension leave her shoulders.

"This is just between you and me. Let Sunny go."

"I have no intention of harming your friend or her child. I only want you, Chavvah. Since the first time I saw you, I knew you would be the last. You have two animals to call. I've seen it. I only need one. You are more connected than anyone I've ever met to the spirits. Your god speaks to you, he changed you, and through your sacrifice, my god will change me. Your skin will be my transformation."

From my vantage by the fridge, I was parallel to Sunny. When she got her wrists free, I had to fight to keep my pulse from pounding out of my chest. My brave, brave friend, who had more heart than sense at times, was a fighter, and if she could fight, so could I. But first, I had to help her get away.

I yanked at the refrigerator doors, using my body to rattle it from its place.

"What are you doing?" The man had a knife in his hand now. The curved skinning blade I'd seen in Sunny's vision. Oh, Jesus. I prayed I'd get out of this with my skin intact.

I screamed. I howled. I wailed. I made so much noise the rafters should have been falling around my ears as I jerked on the cuffs, dragging the fridge out of its place by a few feet. My wrists were shredded where the unforgiving metal dug into them.

The man shouted, "Stop!" as he raced to me, grabbing me from behind. "You're ruining it. You're ruining everything!" He lifted me from the ground, and I threw my head back, slamming into his forehead. He kept one arm around me while he yanked my hair until I could feel the skin pull away from my scalp. I cried out, this time with pain.

I saw spots, which happens when you get your bell rung, but a loud, sharp *thwap* sounded, and the monster staggered back. Sunny was holding a cast iron skillet, the one I'd given her as a Christmas present. It was ten pounds of deadly, and she was wielding it like a Samurai.

"Run, Sunny! Take Jude and run!"

The killer was already coming to his knees, a fierce growl tearing from his lips. Was he shifting? Goddamn it! I was still tied to the large appliance, and Sunny and Jude would be helpless.

"Go!" I screamed when he shoved Sunny back before she could get in another hit. I kicked out, landing a solid blow to the side of his knee. He dropped to the ground with a howl of pain. He grabbed my foot and yanked, pulling my feet from under me, and in the process, hanging me by the hands.

Luckily, it had been enough time for Sunny to grab the baby and run out the side door. *Good girl!*

The man crawled over to me, his words a snarling, raspy tangle of rage. "You think you're tough? You won't think so for long."

My wrists burned, and my head throbbed, but I looked him in the eye, getting my first close-up glimpse of the color. Brown. I sneered, rivulets of blood running to my eyes. "I am tough. If you think I'm going to cry or beg you for any goddamn thing, you can keep on waiting."

He slapped me.

"Is that all you have?"

He put his knife to my cheek. "I think your smart mouth will be the first thing I slice off. Too bad, because it's such a pretty mouth."

I shivered and turned away from him. I prayed Billy Bob would show up. Or, if not him, at least some kind of cavalry. At least, Sunny was out. *Please, Sunny, find yourself a big hole and hide.* This guy's partner was out there somewhere, and I hoped my friend wasn't running straight into his arms.

You are strong, child. You are mine.

I don't know why I felt relieved hearing Brother Wolf, but I did. It wasn't like he could do anything for me, but it was nice not being alone.

I heard a truck engine. His partner? They had to kill me before the full moon. Hadn't he said that? I curled my legs up under me to take pressure off my wrists.

Another vehicle roared to stop, then another and another. I cast a glance at my captor. "I think you're in trouble now, bud."

He stood up from his squat and stalked to the window. The skins covering him made a hissing-like noise when they moved, that made them seem alive. "Son of a bitch!" He turned on me, his hand shaking as he waved his blade. "I told you to come alone."

"And I did." Idiot.

"No," he said, shaking his head. "No. This has to happen. Has to. I can't wait." He was rambling now. He took a deep breath and sharpened his focus on me. "I can't wait," he said with an eerie calm.

He pulled a vial filled with a brown liquid from beneath his skin cloak and shook it at me. The oil substance dribbled down my face, choking me with the scent of sassafras. He began to chant as he raised his hands, curved blade up, and slowly walked toward me.

A tingle of pleasure rippled along my skin. I was turning. Oh, shit. He was calling my animal! Which meant, he planned to kill me now.

"Brother Wolf!" I cried out.

Reach for me, sister, he answered. I rose up so I could reach my pocket and yanked the eight-point star from where it rested and squeezed it tight. It pulsed with power against my skin. I stretched my mind, searching with my thoughts, until I could not only hear Brother Wolf's howl, I could see him.

The killer caught me, yanking me to him. Suddenly, the colors of the world around me exploded as if I were in some fairy realm. It was so much like the *aether* where Brother Wolf existed, only I was still in Sunny's green and chocolate brown kitchen.

Weirdly, I could smell the pungent earthiness of the nearby woods. The rising moon called to me, and it felt incredible. I could not only smell everything, but I could also detect and sort each scent. I imagined what was happening to me was like a software upgrade, only without all the glitches. The cuffs holding me burst apart. I looked down at my paws. They were huge and…black, the color of pitch.

Brother Wolf? What's happening?

You are becoming.

Great. Becoming what?

It didn't matter now. Saving myself before this bastard could turn me into sushi was the most important task. Which, it turned out, was less a problem than I imagined. I must have looked pretty effing scary, because, by the time I'd completed the shift, he'd ran out the back door.

About that same time, Billy Bob burst through the front. He took one look at me, his eyes wide and his mouth grim. Unfettered fury vibrated along his skin. He had a gun in his hand, and I watched as he raised it in my direction. I turned my head to see if the killer had come back.

Nope.

Billy Bob was pointing the gun at me! Holy crap.

"Don't shoot!" I said. Then snapped my muzzle shut. What should have come out of my mouth was a series of whines and barks, but instead, I was speaking like a human. "Doc," I said. "It's me, Chavvah. Put the gun down."

Why wasn't I turning back? *Brother Wolf?*

He didn't answer. *Great time to check out!* Ugh.

Behind Billy Bob, Babe came running in, along with Sheriff Taylor, Farraday, Thompson, and Connelly, Dominic Tartan, Chance Lowry, Willy Boden, and Hans Fisk.

"Whoa!" Willy threw up her hands. "What in the hell is that thing?"

"Oh, Jesus," I muttered.

"It talks!" Connelly said.

"Score one for the squirrel," I said.

He frowned. "How do you know what I am?"

"I can smell your nuts."

He sniffed.

"I'm kidding, Michael." I took a step closer to the group. They all took a wary step back, except Billy Bob. *That's my man!* "Is Sunny okay?"

"Yes," Billy Bob said. "We found her up on the road with Jude. Ruth and Ed took her into town. She's going to stay at their place tonight."

"Oh, thank heavens." It would be dark soon, and all the little creatures and some really large ones would be scurrying about. I watched Hans Fisk fidget under my sweeping gaze of the room. In this group was a killer, and now I knew whom. "Sheriff, arrest Chance Lowry."

"What?" The accused scoffed at me. "I know you've had a hard night, but that doesn't give you the right to make false accusations." He took a step back toward the door. Farraday and Thompson blocked his way.

"I can't arrest the man on the say-so of a ginormous black wolf," the sheriff said.

Dominic Tartan moved with quick efficiency, pulling handcuffs from god-knows-where and slapped them on Lowry's wrists before he could protest. "I don't have the same constraints," he said.

When the sheriff and the deputies moved around him, he pulled his wallet out of his back pocket and flashed a badge.

"I'm FBI. I've been tracking the killings for almost a decade now. I've been close. I knew the killers were based out of Kansas, and that they spree killed during the Tri-Council Jubilee each year, but they've never been this public. I gave the information to Willy to pass along to you."

So he was Willy's contact with the FBI. "It was to be their last time," I said. "Chance and Randy were onto their end game." The laugh, the one that I'd heard, had been Randy's. I remembered all the clues he'd left me, how he was a handyman, how he had a tattoo he'd like to show me. The vain part of me would have liked to believe that some of the flirtings had been real, but it had all been part of a plan to try and get me alone.

"Their dad owns a locksmith shop. It made it awful handy for them to break into places easily... like my restaurant."

"Jacob Lowry had pressed for Peculiar as a location this year," Willy said. "Is he involved?"

I shrugged, which was hard to do with large furry shoulders. "Someone needs to get Randy."

"He's probably shifted and is miles from here," Hans Fisk said. "How can we get to him before the full moon?"

Chance laughed. I growled and snapped in his face. He shut up then. "He can't shift," I said. I'd realized it when he was holding Jude. "That's what all this was about. All this tragedy."

"But I saw him earlier," Tyler Thompson said. "He turned into a coyote."

I shook my head. "No. You saw Chance turn. Randy wasn't with us. He was here with Sunny." My stomach hurt as I thought about what he could have done to her. What he'd planned to do me.

"Why are you in this form, Chavvah?" Sheriff Taylor asked.

I didn't respond because I didn't have any answers.

Babe snapped his fingers and walked across the room to me. "I knew it was you!"

My tongue lolled out the side of my mouth. I swished my tail at him, whacking him in the back. "Duh."

He wrapped his arms around my neck. "Thanks, Sis. Thanks for keeping my family safe."

"Our family," I said. I looked back to the group. "Find Randy. No one is safe as long as that psychopath is out there, and in less than an hour, we're all going to be mindless instinctual animals, and he's going to be a human running around with a really sharp hunting knife."

Sheriff Taylor gestured to Connelly. "Run Tartan into town with the prisoner. We need to get Lowry locked in a cell before dark. Do it fast."

"You got it," Connelly said. He nodded to me. "Uh, Chav. Glad to see you're..." He shook his head. The sheriff glared at him. "Let's go, Tartan." He grabbed Chance by one arm and Dom took the other.

Undercover FBI. I should have known.

The sheriff had already started directing everyone else to go out and search. Billy Bob walked over to me. He stood disturbingly close, leaned in and peered into my eyes. "It's really you."

"I think so." I licked his face leaving a large slug's trail of saliva along his cheek and over his nose. "Turnabout's fair play, Doc." I laughed. It sounded strange. "I don't know how to get back to human."

"Then I will be a wolf with you."

"I'm bigger than you."

"I have a thing for big girls." The left corner of his mouth tugged up. "Why do you look like Brother Wolf?"

"I don't know. The bastard won't talk to me." Having Billy Bob near me eased my fear, but I still didn't feel safe. Not with Randy out there. "His mother. Their mother. She warped them. I think she made them believe if they could access the spirits, that Randy could be a shifter." I recalled how he'd talked about her bathing him with sassafras. "Their rings are eight point stars. Not two overlaid cubes. I'm pretty sure they've been messing with forces on the other side for a long time."

"Being a non-shifter in a shifter home has consequences."

Was he thinking about baby Jude? "Sunny's human. It won't be the same for her and Babe with their children."

"I didn't mean to imply that it would, Chav." He stroked the fur on my neck. "Come back to me."

"I should be out there hunting him down."

"You've done enough."

"You should be out there, too."

"I'm not leaving you. I'm not letting you out of my sight."

About that time, the kitchen door flew open. Randy Lowry stood there—his eyes wild with madness as he trained a 9mm gun at Billy Bob and me.

"You've destroyed everything!" I saw the flash of the muzzle, the deafening blast as he pulled the trigger, the bullet ripping through the air heading for me as if in slow motion.

"No," Billy Bob shouted. He shoved me aside, and I watched as the deadly projectile slammed into his chest.

I roared, a frenzy of emotions overwhelming all my senses. Billy Bob had thrown himself in front of a bullet for me, and I would not let it go unanswered. Randy turned, the skins sliding off his back exposing his hideous eight-point star tattoo, the one I'd seen in Sunny's vision. I leaped on top of him, his screams barely penetrating the red rage coursing through my veins. In this form, I had him easily pinned to the floor.

"No," he cried out. "Please!"

I leaned in close, my breath mussing his hair. I opened my mouth, my jaw unhinged, widening like that of a man-eating python.

"Wait. Wait!" he exclaimed as my saliva dribbled on his face.

"I'm going to transform you, human. I'm going to grant your wish."

Okay, the words came out of my mouth, or rather the big black wolf's mouth, because I hadn't said the words. Apparently, I'd stopped being in charge of the body I'd inhabited. I tried not to gag as we, because I was definitely a *we* now, swallowed Randy Lowry down like a bitter pill. In less than a minute, he was…in my belly.

He tasted like chicken.

Not really. I hadn't tasted anything. It was as if I hadn't really been a part of Randy's demise at all. I heard a moan, and it brought me back to the present. Billy Bob! I ran to him, sliding the last couple of feet until I could cradle him in my arms.

I didn't feel afraid for myself anymore. Chance Lowry was in prison, and well, we won't rehash the whole people-eating trick I'd just performed on his non-shifting twin. Now, I was only afraid to lose Billy Bob.

"Hang in there, Doc." I put my hand over the wound in his chest. God, there was so much blood. "Stay with me. Please, stay with me."

He put his hand on mine. "You're you again," he said, his voice raspy and weak. "You're so beautiful."

I looked at my hand, all skin and no fur. "I hadn't even noticed. Can you shift? Will that help?" I was still in my clothes, which meant it hadn't been a traditional shift, and the eight-point star was still in my hand. I pressed it over his wound, hoping the energy from it would help stop the bleeding somehow.

"I don't know. I've lost a lot of blood," he said.

He was so pale my heart wanted to seize. "You're strong. Too strong to die."

"Chavvah."

"No," I said. "You don't get to die."

"I am glad for you, Chavvah. I am thankful..." His voice faded as his eyes fluttered to a close.

"No!" I shouted. He was breathing, but it was a quick, shallow panting. The first thing I wanted to do was call my mom. She was a nurse. I needed a nurse. Or a doctor. But the doctor was not fucking in!

Be calm, little wolf.

Shut the hell up! If there was ever a moment to panic, now was the time.

Sister, you are strong. You are brave. Be calm.

This was not how the story ended. Billy Bob and I had a lifetime of stories to create. Brother Wolf could just suck it. "You be helpful," I cried. "Be helpful."

I am, little wolf.

That was the second time he called me little wolf. Oh shit. "I'm a wolf!"

I could feel the pleasure of my guardian spirit.

"Sue me," I said. "This better work."

I moved my hand off the hole in Billy Bob's chest, gathered all the saliva in my mouth until it was full then spit on the wound. The white froth mingled with his blood, but nothing happened. There was no magical healing like I'd seen when Billy Bob applied his juju to injuries. Of course, his was usually in some kind of salve or balm. Maybe I was missing a second key ingredient.

"Brother Wolf!"

Be patient.

"Doc," I said. "Billy Bob Smith, come back to me. I promise I won't be so stubborn. Just please don't leave me." Fat tears along with some pretty awful snot streaked my face. I lay across his stomach, my hand back on the wound. "Brother Wolf, please help me. Save him. Save him."

"He doesn't have to," the low, familiar voice of a certain werewolf shaman doc said. "I…I'm recovering."

I wiped my runny nose on the bottom of his shirt before I sat up. He moved up on his elbow. A grimace told me he might be better, but he was still in pain. I didn't let him get too far before I kissed him. I didn't go all passion-diva on him because he groaned at one point, and it wasn't because it felt good.

"Sorry," I said. "I just didn't think I'd ever have a chance to do that again."

"You're going to have the rest of our long, long lives." He gave me a crooked grin. The wound on his chest looked raw, but it had stopped bleeding. He poked his finger about an inch or two in and plucked out a bullet. "How?"

"I'm part wolf now," I shrugged sheepishly. "I have my ways."

"You spit on me."

"Yep. A great big loogie."

He stroked my hair back from my face. "Thank you."

"You took a bullet for me. It was the least I could do."

"And I would again and again."

"Don't you fucking dare," I said. "I prefer you among the living."

"I prefer you alive as well."

"Then we're agreed. Neither of us takes a bullet again."

"This is going to be an interesting life with you."

"A laugh riot, I'm sure." I could feel the heaviness of the rising moon and the gentle tingle along my skin. "It's almost time. Do you have your phone on you?"

Billy Bob dug it out of his pocket. I pulled up a text and added contacts as quickly as I could. I typed in: **All is well. Bad guy dead. Happy full moon.**

"You're like a ninja with that thing." He kissed me softly, sweetly, and so sexily it made my hair sizzle.

"We're not having sex as wolves."

"It is a full moon. We'll be running on pure instinct, baby."

"Not this girl." I laughed then, and it felt really great.

"Did you really eat a full grown person in a few bites?"

"Uhm, I don't think there was much biting going on. It was more like I swallowed him whole."

Billy Bob raised his brows, suddenly very interested.

I smacked him hard across the chest.

"Ow," he said, rubbing his hand over the healing wound.

"I'm sorry!"

He grabbed me in his arms and pulled me onto his lap. "I really do love you, Chavvah Adine Trimmel."

"Who told you my middle name?"

"A doctor has his ways."

"Sunny."

"Yep."

"I love you right back, William Robert Smith."

He cringed. "I won't call you Adine again, as long as you never call me William Robert ever again. It was my father's name, not mine."

"I'd rather call you Doc, anyhow." I booped his nose with the tip of my finger. "My favorite character in Snow White."

"You can call me Doc or Sleepy or Horny."

"Is that the eighth dwarf?"

He smiled and leaned his head back, the gray in his eyes swirling. "I love the magic of the moon."

I'd never thought of the full moon as magic. It had always been like getting my period—a monthly visitor I had to deal with no matter how unpleasant the side effects. At this moment, I understood what Billy Bob meant, and in many ways, I'd become a believer. How else could I explain turning into a big, scary spirit guardian? That shit had nothing to do with biology.

You are learning, child.

It pleased me that he thought so. The air rippled around us. "It's coming," I said.

I hoped his wolf loved mine as much as he loved me and vice versa.

Not in that way! Though we'd be animals, so no judging.

The change was swift for both of us, and when our beasts had completely replaced us, our human thoughts faded.

Chapter 15

"SO," MY SUPPOSED BFF for life, walk through fire, always have my back, girls before squirrels, best friend said. "Let me get this straight, and stop me if I go off track. A spirit guardian, a god-like creature, for lack of a better term, gave you the ability to possess his big, black bad ass wolf form, and you chugged back a serial killer like he was a two-dollar shot on ladies' night at the Gin and Bear It?"

I pursed my lips and wiggled them back and forth before answering. "That's about the truth of it." The eight-point star, it turned out, was a conduit right to the *aether*. At least, for a spirit-talker. Billy Bob and I planned to play around with it in his sweat lodge, and no, that wasn't a euphemism. Apparently, I was an unnatural phenomenon when it came to matters of the spirit.

"It's a pretty tall tale, Chav. Are you taking lessons from the Johnson twins?" Ruth Thompson said.

"I believe you," Willy Boden said. "It's too crazy not to be real."

"That and four bucks will buy you a cup of coffee," Sunny said.

"I don't know where you buy your coffee," Ruth said, "but you're getting ripped off.

"I miss a good gourmet double mocha cinnamon cappuccino with extra froth and sprinkle of cardamom," I said, visualizing the extra froth.

"Mmmm," Sunny agreed. The mmm sound always meant consensus. "I could really go for a soy chai latte mega venti." She thwapped me with the back of her hand. "Damn it, Chav. Now I'm going to crave that the whole time I'm pregnant."

I grinned. "I'll order the ingredients and make them special just for you."

She patted her still flat belly. "Thank you. Your new niece will thank you, too." She wiggled her brows.

Ruth and Willy squealed with delight. Ruth said, "I can't wait to shop for her. There are so many cute baby clothes for girls. Not like when my girls were little." A wistful expression made her princess features even more fairytale-like.

"Oh, you have to invite me back when the baby is born," Willy said.

I liked her so much, which is why I didn't tell her that I had suspected her brother of being one of the killers. I wanted to get this friendship off to a healthy start. It turned out that Hans had been surly and contemptuous because he'd been dating Bethany Hilliard off and on for a year, and he made a business deal with her on the side to supply sassafras for the Jubilee. She'd made a side deal with several furniture crafters, including Elton Brown for the wood.

Which explained why Elton was able to make all those awesome pieces.

Still, I think Hans would have been okay getting screwed over in the deal if she hadn't dropped him like a rock to pursue Billy Bob. Oh, and the tattoo on his arm was a five-point star, not an eight.

I put my hand on Ruth's knee. "How's Michele doing today?"

Ruth shook her head. "Oh, she's fine. I think it's going to be a while before Ed lets her out of his sight." She cast her eyes down to her piece of peach cobbler. "I can't believe how close we came…"

Sunny took her hand in sympathy. "Poor Michele," she said. A wicked grin played on her lips. "Jo Jo's going to have to become a second-story man to court her."

"Don't even start with that," Ruth said, but she laughed. "He's not a bad kid."

"A man," Willy said.

All three of us gave her side-eye.

She shrugged. "He's nineteen isn't he, and a cutie at that."

"He's too young for you," I told the vivacious redhead.

"And he's taken at the moment," Ruth said protectively.

We all laughed then. For the first time in days, I could breathe. The first night of the full moon was over, the Tri-Council was having their meeting, and I got to spend the afternoon with friends. Willy had known Dom was undercover FBI because he used to work security for the council with her until he decided to integrate. That's why they'd had a falling out. I personally think his integration had more to do with tracking those of our kind who threatened to expose us to the world. With the FBI, he had more resources and was better able to follow what might be shifter related versus human related.

Jacob Lowry resigned as President of the Council when he found out what his sons had been doing with their free time. Bethany Hilliard was named the new president. Yuck. The news had left a real bad taste in my mouth.

"Oh," Sunny said. She reached down to the play blanket and picked up Jude. "Guess who turned into the cutest little coyote pup last night?"

"Oh. My. God. Sunny! Way to bury the lead!" I grabbed Jude from her arms and cuddled him. "What a little genius. You are a bright and shining star, Jude."

He put his hand in my mouth and giggled in response.

"Babe was so proud," Sunny said, her eyes glittery with emotion. "So proud."

"Well." Ruth stood up. "This calls for celebratory ice cream to go with the cobbler."

"I really am falling in love with you, Ruth," Willy said, as she scooped up her last bite of crust. "I'll take more of both."

Ruth practically danced with pleasure to her freezer.

Sunny leaned over to me. "Now that all the niceties are over, I want details."

I played stupid. "I don't know what you mean."

"I bet he's really good at the horizontal make-it-rain dance."

"That's not a saying."

"He probably knows how to slide into home plate for a double touchdown and a two-point goal."

I concentrated on the baby I was holding. "You're mixing your sports metaphors."

"I bet he makes you scream so loud it makes dolphins on the west coast blush."

"You're being ridiculous."

"Tell me all about how his wooly mammoth avoided the ice age by hiding in your heated cave."

"Sunny!" Ruth exclaimed. Willy laughed so hard tears ran down her face.

Frankly, I nearly peed my pants. "You are truly awful! Besides, there is nothing wooly about his mammoth as you well know since you got a really good look at it the other morning when you went all Peeping Tom at his bedroom window."

"I'm not a Peeping Tom," she said, managing to sound genuinely hurt. She glanced my way, her gaze meeting mine, a sly grin growing out at the edges of her mouth. "Though, wowza, you're right. There is nothing wooly about that genuine mammoth."

Willy hooted. I blushed. Ruth had the good sense to pretend we were talking about the weather.

I glared at Sunny. "Didn't you say you were meeting Babe and some of the council members for lunch?"

"Crap. Yes." She looked at her watch. "I need to get going. I'm already late."

Her shirt was a pretty shade of kiwi green, a color that really brought out her eyes. I held up Jude. "I think the baby's hungry." I followed this line with just the right high-pitched cry.

"Chavvah!" Sunny's hands covered her leaking boobs, which did little to stop Niagara Falls from whooshing down her chest.

"You're welcome," I said. "Tell my bro I say hey."

She grabbed a receiving blanket and draped it across her chest. "I'll get you for this, chick."

I smiled sweetly. "You'll try."

"It's a good thing I love you." She took Jude from me.

"Ditto that," I told her, and with all my might, I believed it. I thanked my stars every day that Sunny Haddock, make that Trimmel, loved me. It was one of those rare miracles you get in life.

"Knock, knock," said the voice of my sexy ass man. He stood in the back door. "Am I interrupting you ladies, or is this a no-wooly-mammoths-allowed zone?"

The look on Sunny's face, the red-hot embarrassment crawling up her cheeks onto her ears, had made all her taunting worth it. "Uhm." She nodded down to Jude. "I'll see you all later. Baby needs feeding."

Billy Bob held out his hand to me, and I took it, so happy to let him pull me into his arms. He walked me out the kitchen door into Ruth's lush back yard and pulled me in close, his fingers pushing my hair away from my ear. He leaned down and whispered, "I have a certain dinosaur looking for a hot spot to hide out for a while."

My eyes widened.

He winked. "I feel another ice age coming on."

Willy said, "Therianthrope hearing, you all, and the windows are open. Just in case you thought you were alone."

"Jealous," I teased.

"You bet," she said.

I jumped up and looped my legs around Billy Bob's waist. "Let's go make some dolphins blush."

The growl vibrating up his chest filled me with such anticipation.

"You make me so goddamn happy, woman."

"I don't plan to stop."

"I'll hold you to it because I am only mating once, and it's for life."

"Is that a proposal?" Sunny came staggering through the back door still wrapped up in the blanket and carrying baby Jude.

"Sunny!"

Billy Bob cupped my face. His flirty expression became more serious. "Chavvah. I have waited a lifetime for you, and I don't want to wait a minute more." He reached down into his pocket, which brushed against some very sensitive bits of mine. When his hand came back up, he held a small box.

"Holy shit," Sunny said. "This really is a proposal!"

He flipped it open with his thumb. Inside was a dark gold band with two circles holding two large diamonds. "I love you, Chavvah. Under the sun, under the moon, and every moment in between, I love you. You'd make me the happiest man alive if you would do me the honor of marrying me."

"I…" I hadn't expected this. Not so soon. It had taken Babe a few months to propose to Sunny. "I…"

"Yes!" Sunny screamed. "For God sake, yes!"

I met his silver gaze and smiled. "What she said." I kissed him. "I do so love you." He slid the ring on my finger, and it fit perfectly. I held out my hand to admire the magnificence and to show it off to the girls. "When did you get this?"

"About six months ago."

"Seriously?"

"As soon as I knew I loved you, I wanted to be ready for the moment you loved me back."

"You're about two years late then."

He smiled. "Well, I've caught up now."

"You sure have." I kissed him again then jumped down to give the threesome of happy ladies a closer look.

"It's so beautiful," Ruth said, wiping a tear from her eye.

"Lucky devil," Willy added.

Sunny hugged me hard. "You're moving to the big house!"

"You make it sound like prison."

"It is marriage," Willy said.

"Okay, okay." This sweet moment was turning ugly. "Take me home, Doc. We have an extinction to prevent."

He raised a brow, to which I mouthed. "Wooly mammoth."

The End

ABOUT THE AUTHOR

USA Today Bestselling author Reneé George has been an Army medic, a nurse, a website designer, a small press editor, an artist, and a teacher, but writing is her true passion. Reneé loves creating stories around quirky characters solving big mysteries in small, rural towns (BEST JOB EVER!). She and her family live in a rural Missouri town, sharing their home with two dogs and a very independent cat.

ACKNOWLEDGEMENTS

I'd like to thank the usual suspects for making this book even more awesome! First, my BFF Michele Bardsley, who is a kick ass editor and great hand holder. Secondly, my sister Robbin for an honest, *Come to Jesus*, critique from a readers POV, my BFF Dakota Cassidy, who keeps me on writing track by sitting on the phone with me for four or five hours three nights a week, and for all the fans of the series who make it fun to keep writing these wonderful Peculiar shifters.

I'd also like to thank Michelle the Magnificent for helping me to stay calm (which is a bigger deal than you can imagine). Also, I can't forget to mention my husband, who works hard all week long so I can stay home and pursue my writing full time, and my son (aka the man-child), who makes dinner every night, so I don't have to!!! It's a huge load off. I love you all, and my life would be a total dud without you!

www.ingramcontent.com/pod-product-compliance
Lightning Source LLC
Chambersburg PA
CBHW070910180626
46817CB00003B/1002